Wolf's Bane

M.S. Gardner

Winner of the
Moon Meridian Novella Award

©2025 M.S. Gardner
Cover ©2025 Danny Weddle

-First Edition

Publisher's Cataloguing-in-Publication Data

Gardner, M.S.
   Wolf's bane / written by M.S. Gardner
   ISBN: 978-1-953932-36-5

1. Fiction: General 2. Fiction: Literary I. Title II. Author

Library of Congress Control Number: 2025931867

Praise for M.S. Gardner

"M.S. Gardner is a force of nature. With steady patience and great skill, Gardner weaves a gritty and haunting tale that lures us into sharp-toothed thickets where nothing is as safe as we might think. Her prose balances elegantly on the razor's edge of restraint and mystery as past secrets brood beneath the surface tension of the present. Wolf's Bane is a story I won't soon forget."
-Gina Ochsner, author of *The Hidden Letters Of Velta B*

"*Wolf's Bane*, a gripping psychological tale, had me from foreshadowing to finale. Gardner's style captures the story's characters so well and develops the plot so perfectly that I was compelled to not only relish the narrative but savor the dialogue as well."
-J. Nolan White, author of the *Pedigree Nation* series.

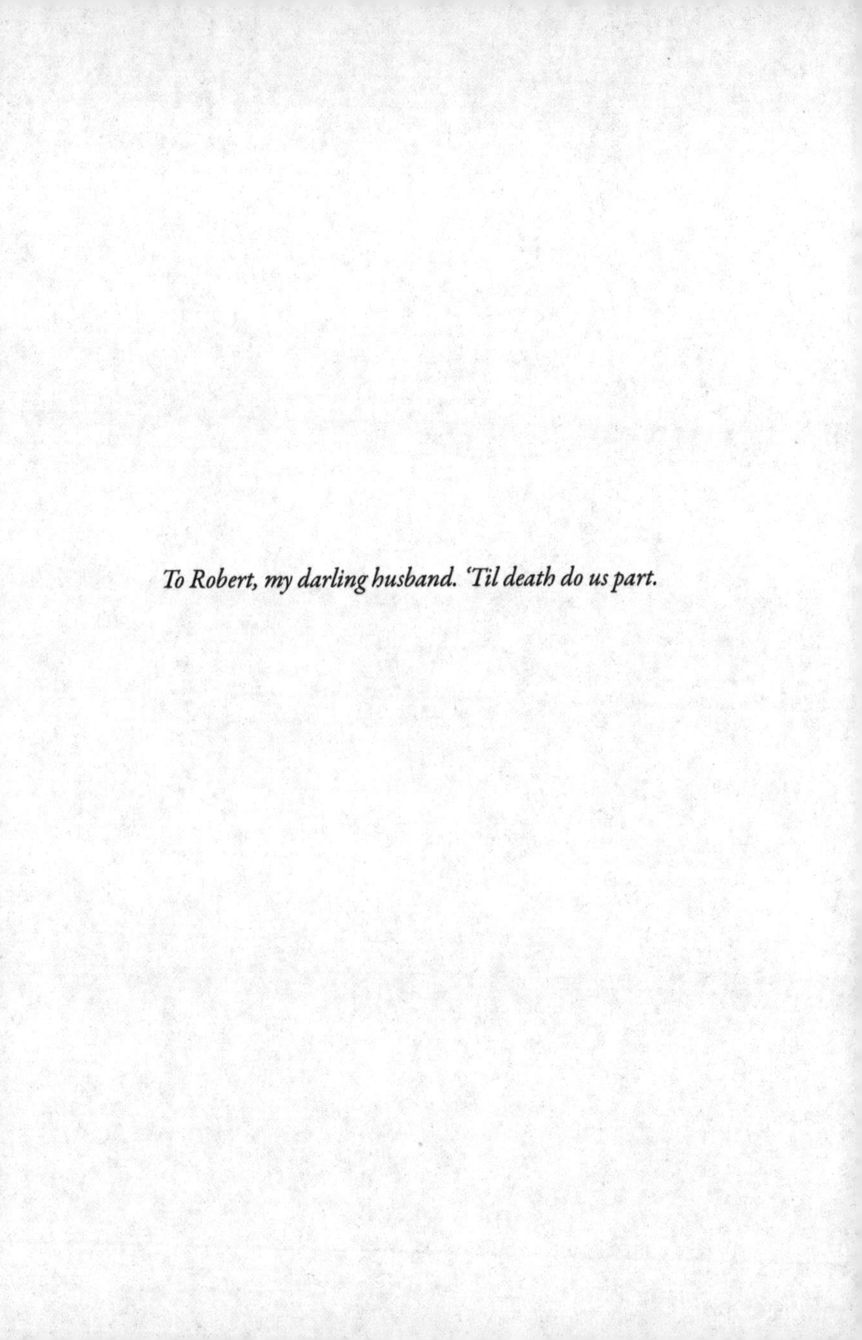

To Robert, my darling husband. 'Til death do us part.

I

SHE FELT IT COMING, sensed it circling her like a predator, in stealth, closing the distance between itself and its prey, the fate appointed to all men, the only sure thing in life—the end of it, when the Angel of Death descends and reaps the soul, the soul receiving its everlasting reward or everlasting punishment. She was an old woman, had been granted much more than the allotted three-score and ten years prescribed in the Good Book. With all of her affairs in order, she was ready, even more than ready, verging on eagerness.

Except for the nagging, persistent seed of doubt in her heart, if that *one* sin, a sin committed so very, very long ago, one awful sin done with a pure heart, a sin committed to punish a greater sin, was truly forgiven. All those decades ago, she'd decided she'd gladly risk damnation and the everlasting fires of Hell to spare her granddaughter. For a long time, it—her sin—didn't trouble her. There were great spans of time when she'd even forgotten what she'd done. The decades accumulated, piled up like dust clumps under a couch.

Every morning of late, when she woke up, she felt Death inch closer, so close his icy breath raised the wispy hairs on the back of her neck, chilling the marrow of her bones, and the seed of doubt grew larger, swelling, ready to burst from its shell and spread like kudzu through her soul.

She'd considered confessing, turning herself in—she was an old woman, what could they do to her? She didn't fear jail—no, she feared the repercussions, the shockwave of shame that might engulf her granddaughter. Such a long, long time ago. Did Penny even remember? They say children forget. What good could be had by owning up now?

But still, as Death stalked her, creeping closer every day, shadowing her footsteps, the burden to confess grew heavier, like a millstone hung around her neck. God forgive her, but she'd even considered going to the Catholic church, getting in one of them funny booths, and pouring out her sin to the stranger on the other side. Except, he weren't no stranger, was he? Everybody knew everybody in Osyka, and you couldn't count on nobody to keep their mouth shut, and she didn't trust a Papist.

Maybe pride held her back from telling somebody. She'd lived long enough to know all too well how deceitful the human heart was, how even the purest motive had a dark underbelly. If Reverend Phips were still alive, she might could work up the courage to tell him, but he'd passed onto glory some six months ago—or was it seven?—and she hadn't taken to the new fella who'd replaced Reverend Phips. The new pastor was too young, told 'feel good' stories that tickled the ears instead of preaching from the Word of God. She had a hard time remembering the new pastor's name. So her sin remained, unconfessed to mortal man, and for months it worried her and festered under her skin like a deep splinter she couldn't extract.

One unseasonably cold January Mississippi morning, when she woke up from a troubled sleep, it came to her, an epiphany, what she needed to do. She'd confess to Penny, tell Penny what she'd done all those decades ago. How much did Penny remember from that first summer— how old had she been? Five? Six?

But Penny was a grown woman now. She hadn't seen her granddaughter in ages, not since Penny had graduated from high school, and she'd taken a Greyhound bus from Mississippi to Richmond, Virginia to see Penny get her diploma. In all those years since, Penny hadn't forgotten her—she still called her granny regularly, sent little gifts, trinkets, and knickknacks from all the places she visited. These mementos held pride of place on the fireplace mantle. And she took care of her granny, in her own way, even though she lived so far away. Penny was a doctor—Lord, why couldn't she remember what kind?—and made good money and had all her granny's bills sent to her office in Seattle, just so the old woman's Social Security check would stretch further. Her Penny was a good girl; she'd understand.

The matter was settled—she'd confess her sin to the person she'd committed it for. Though, not on the phone. She couldn't bring herself to talk about it, afraid Penny might ask her why, ask too many questions, and she didn't want to speak such filth.

And so, on that frigid morning, she eased her ancient bones out of bed, dressed for the day, shuffled down the hallway, her slippers scuffing against the hardwood floor toward the stairwell. She navigated the stairs with care, guiding her way down, one hand on the banister, the other hand braced against the opposite wall, taking the steps one-by-one until she reached the bottom and took one step into the living room.

The first thing she laid eyes on was the recliner, a hideous mud-brown eyesore, and a shiver seized her, shook her like a dog with a rat in its mouth. She loathed that recliner, had hated it from the moment her husband had bought it, first because she'd thought it was as ugly as sin, but then for other reasons she cared not to remember. Folks who'd drop by to visit thought she kept it for sentimental reasons, wouldn't let anyone sit in it out of respect for her late husband. But no. She kept it as a reminder, her thorn of the flesh.

As she stood in the threshold at the bottom of the stairs holding onto the doorframe for support as her legs quaked, she forced herself to look at the recliner, to stare it down. The seat of the recliner still held the impression of his backside, the material compressed and molded from years of use. In her mind's eye, she saw him—he'd been a big man, tall, and in his last years, fat, his belly as round as a barrel and taut. Everything about him in life had been huge, especially his appetites, and even death hadn't shrunken him, as it did all others, on his last day on Earth, stretched out in his recliner, his mouth agape in horror, his eyes staring into eternity, his long, thick fingers clutching the arms of the chair in vain as Death had dragged away his sin-bloated soul, leaving behind his vessel of ample flesh.

Outside, a gust of wind shook the oak tree out front; the branches raking against the roof sounded like a death rattle. A chill rippled through her, her weak knees threatened to buckle, and she looked away. She averted her eyes as she passed into the kitchen to fix her coffee and sat at the kitchen table, working up the gumption to complete her mission. She had her coffee, read her daily devotional, and once her fingers, stiff and swollen, knobby with arthritis, warmed and loosened up some, she got out pen and paper.

It took over an hour to write the letter, for she had to pause when weeping fits came over her, but once it was finished, the burden of her heart rolled away, just like in the hymn, and she thought she'd float up and fly away from the lightness. Now, how to get it to Penny. She didn't want to mail it—what if it got lost in the mail and someone else read it? She didn't want to leave it with the lawyer. After writing her will years ago, a simple document leaving all her earthly possessions, including the house, to Penny, she'd had no more use for the lawyer. She held a general distrust of lawyers, even if they were a necessary evil, and this was personal family business.

But who could she trust? And the answer came before the question even finished forming in her mind. Duncan. She trusted Duncan; she'd leave it with him to give to Penny once she was dead and gone. She folded the letter carefully into thirds, smoothing the creases with the side of her thumb, slipped it into an envelope, sealed it, wrote Penny's name on the front, and slid the letter into the back of her Bible—the safest place she knew.

She hefted herself from the chair and went to the phone to call Duncan but found she couldn't exactly remember the number. Shaking her head at her forgetfulness, she shuffled to the fridge and retrieved his business card, grabbing her readers off the table on her way back to the phone. Even with her readers on, she had to squint to make out the numbers as she dialed the rotary phone.

The line rang three times, clicked, and Duncan's voice came through: *Need a handyman who can? Duncan CAN! Leave your name and number and I'll get—*

She hung up without leaving a message. She hated talking into those answering machines. No matter, more likely than not he'd stop by later in the day or sometime the next. She put his card back on the fridge, fixing it in place with a mini peach-shaped magnet, when the phone rang. She answered, hoping it was Duncan, but it was one of the church ladies. She spent a good while on the phone, working out the details for the monthly Sunday potluck, and by the time she hung up, she forgot about the letter.

She went to bed that evening and slept her last night on the earth.

II

PENNY FIDDLED WITH THE AIR CONDITIONER KNOBS in the rental car, trying to get the cabin cooler, and added items to her mental list of 'things to never do again.' She'd never fly NW again—what should've been a seven-hour flight from Seattle to Gulfport-Biloxi had turned into a ten-hour ordeal. She'd never rent a car from *that* company again—they'd downgraded her to an economy car due to some 'computer error,' didn't have any cars in the size she'd wanted, and she'd been too tired to argue with the lady behind the counter for an upgrade to a luxury model at the same price. She'd never listen to a GPS again—for some unfathomable reason, the unnaturally chipper voice in the box had suggested the least time-efficient route from the airport to her destination, and like a sheep, she'd simply turned when told.

She stopped her inner litany. She always told her patients to take responsibility for their actions; she should do the same. *Physician, heal thyself.* The last person to use the GPS must've changed the setting to 'shortest distance' instead of 'shortest time.' If she'd been paying attention to the GPS, instead of stewing over the rental car mix-up, she'd have noticed this sooner. If she hadn't waited until the last minute to book her flight, she could've flown into New Orleans, spent the night there, and headed out in the morning. Staying in Biloxi hadn't appealed to her but would've been an option had she been willing to spend the night in an overpriced casino hotel or in a cheap fleabag motel. At least she'd had the forethought to stop and get some groceries and a few empty liquor boxes, suspecting her options would be limited in the backwoods town where

15

her grandmother had lived, a town no bigger than a speck of fly shit on a map.

It all boiled down to this: she shouldn't have waited six months to deal with her grandmother's estate. She should've dealt with it right after the funeral. Grief took many forms, this she knew, this she preached to her patients as they sat across from her, struggling, some crying, some staring blankly as they spoke, the shock of pain yet to shake their beings, and all the while she'd study them, jotting down the occasional note, flicking her eyes surreptitiously at the small clock on her desk, her face a mask of distant concern as she'd push a tissue box toward them.

An involuntary tic twitched her eyelid. She reached up to rub the spasming muscle. Why hadn't she dealt with things right after the funeral? With a practiced clinical detachment, she mentally stepped back from herself, examining. Was she "stuck" in denial? She wasn't a child—there was no denying her grandmother was dead, no pretending Grandma was in a 'better place' or simply off somewhere to return, someday, soon. So, why wait so long to come back, to execute what made up her grandmother's merger estate? Hell, she hadn't even bothered contacting the electric company to cut off the electricity to the house, though it'd been on a 'to-do' list since the funeral. *Wasn't all this evidence of denial?* she asked herself, probing, but she had no answer, that part of her closed, silent as a sullen child.

How long would she have put it off, if her grandmother's lawyer hadn't pestered the ever living hell out of her for the past month, the town council badgering him, concerned about the house remaining vacant? The lawyer had indicated someone was interested in buying the property, if she wanted to sell it. Did she want to sell it? She didn't want to keep it, that was for sure, but for some reason which she couldn't pinpoint, the prospect of selling the property didn't sit well with her either. It seemed like a betrayal letting a stranger have the house. Her thoughts wandered, branching off, spreading and weaving like brambles, thick and dense as the untamed underbrush of a forest, the long straight stretch of road and surrounding greenery barely registering as a blur as she drove.

The dog appeared out of nowhere, a Border Collie, hunkered down in the overgrown grass and weeds that stretched along the side of the road, watching and waiting, itching and eager to dash out after any passing car, its herding instincts overpowering any sense of danger. Anyone familiar with the stretch of road would've known to watch out for the dog. Anyone driving the speed limit or less would've been able to stop or swerve in time.

But Penny wasn't familiar with the road and was going fifteen miles over the speed limit, distracted by her thoughts, road-blind from the monotonous scenery, weary from the long flight and stress-filled day. A blur of black and white flashed in her peripheral vision, followed by a *thud* and a sharp, quick yelp.

By the time she found a patch of shoulder wide enough to pull over, the dog had disappeared, having crawled back deep into the tall grass to die. For a moment, she considered getting out of the car and finding it but dismissed the thought. Injured animals were dangerous.

She eased the car back onto the road but only drove ten yards before her stomach wrenched and her mouth filled with bile, burning her throat. She stopped the car, opened the door, leaned out the side, and vomited. Stomach acid coated her teeth, stung her nostrils, and she spat several times, swishing sips of bottled water to rinse out her mouth. She blew her nose, found an old menthol cough drop at the bottom of her purse, put the car into drive, and went on.

By the time she made it over the state line and into the edge of town, she'd put the incident out of her mind, focusing on making her way through the meandering streets, the town feeling both foreign and familiar to her, until she pulled up to her grandmother's place. She got out of the car, the humid Mississippi air assaulting her body, her lungs, and she stood for several minutes, scanning the two-story house and the yard. In the summer dusk, the white house looked like tarnished silver. The oak tree in the front yard towered over the house, its branches stretched out to the roof as if to possess it. The screams of cicadas and the chirping of tree frogs filled the evening air, punctuated by the occasional hoot of an owl. A dog barked in the distance.

The last time she'd set foot on the property, she'd been twelve years old, the last summer she'd spend with her grandmother. She hadn't come back to the house after the funeral but had left from the gravesite and driven straight back to the New Orleans airport and waited for her flight—a social faux pas as Grandma's mourners had all gone back to the house for the wake, complete with covered dishes appropriate for the occasion: quick casseroles of tinned chicken or tuna, canned vegetables, and condensed mushroom soup, topped with crushed potato chips or deep-fried onions, and multiple cakes, dozens of cookies, and Jell-O desserts, all standard Southern funeral fare. She'd been back in Seattle a few days when a call came from her grandmother's pastor, his condolences laced with subtle chiding.

She turned away from the house and the memory. She unplugged the GPS and stowed it in the glove box—the rental company would charge an arm and a leg to replace it—then popped open the trunk of the car and unloaded it, setting her carry-on, briefcase, purse, empty liquor boxes, and the few groceries she'd bought on the front porch before entering the house, using a penlight to find the right key to unlock the door.

The house felt abandoned, the air heavy with the odor of disuse and mice, the floor beneath her feet gritty, and when she stepped further in to find the light switch, something *pop-squished* under her shoe. She flipped the light switch. Only one of the bulbs worked in the overhead fixture, bathing the front parlor in a dingy piss-yellow light. She lifted her foot; she'd stepped on a spider.

A coat of dust layered everything. Cobwebs, thick as Spanish moss, festooned the corners of the ceiling, hung like tattered streamers from the blades of the ceiling fan. A pang of guilt, sharp and quick, stabbed her. How often had she talked to her grandma on the phone over the years, making promises to come visit and yet never did? *I'm sorry, Grandma, but I can't make it this year—too many patients, too busy at work, must prepare for X, Y, or Z conference—why don't I fly you here, come visit me?* But Grandma would never come, didn't trust those 'flying contraptions,' and so they had both settled for monthly phone calls all those decades.

She brought everything into the house, left the boxes in the parlor, carried the grocery bags in one hand, the plastic digging into her palms, and pulled her carry-on, with her purse and briefcase stacked precariously on top, behind her, shutting the front door with her foot. At the threshold between the parlor and the living room, she paused. From the parlor, only a sliver of light, weak and pale, bled into the living room, the room cast in darkness. Fear, ancient and dormant, stirred in her, adrenaline rushed into her bloodstream, causing her heart to race, her breathing quick and shallow, and she groped the wall, searching for the light switch.

Relief flooded her when light filled the room. The room was as she remembered it from when she was a child: the overstuffed sofa with its bold cornucopia print and wood accents, a multi-colored crocheted afghan draped over the back, flanked by wood end tables with matching jade-green glass lamps, and a heavy, dark-stained pine coffee table. On the opposite wall, the fireplace, its mantle covered with knickknacks, and tucked in the far corner, an accent chair and a tall, freestanding lamp where Grandma used to sit to crochet or do her embroidery. A T.V. console, the pinnacle of entertainment during its time with its combination of a television, radio, and record player, took up most of the space along the wall, a rabbit-ear antennae and a small, framed print of "Jesus and the little children" centered on the top, a rattan record holder on the floor beside it. The wall between the living room and the kitchen had built-in bookshelves which reached from the floor to the ceiling, and in front of the bookshelves sat her grandfather's recliner, an ugly shit-brown monstrosity, like a huge fat toad from a fairy tale, waiting in the forest to devour little girls who strayed from the path.

Above her, one of the lightbulbs *popped,* and the room dimmed another degree, the noise snapping her back to the present. She left her carry-on at the bottom of the stairs and took everything else into the kitchen, instinctively averting her gaze as she passed the recliner.

She set the grocery bags on the table, along with her briefcase and purse, and emptied the plastic sacks, putting the items away: box of black garbage bags placed on the table, bread stored in the breadbox on the counter, coffee, filters, and a canister of sugar went in the cupboard above. She unwrapped a roll of paper towels and set it on the counter by the coffee pot. She opened the fridge and detected a whiff of decay, the remnants of something having spoiled long ago. A bottle of ketchup and a jar of mustard rattled in the door. The fridge was practically bare: a plastic pitcher of tea, a dark sepia ring at the quarter mark, an unopened carton of orange juice, a can of evaporated milk, the top punctured with two triangular holes and rimmed with yellowed crust. A tin-foiled covered dinner plate, a peek under the foil revealed what looked to be two shriveled pork chops. A Cool-Whip container she dared not open. The crisper drawer contained a bag with a few withered and wrinkled carrots and half a head of cabbage, the core sprouted in hope. She frowned, annoyed—surely one of her grandma's "good Christian friends" could've had the decency to at least clean out the fridge six months ago.

She poured the orange juice and the remains of the tea down the sink, tossing both the pitcher and empty container into a trash bag, followed by the other items left in the fridge, and then tied off the bag and placed it out on the enclosed back porch. After washing her hands, she put up the rest of the groceries she'd bought: three bottles of mediocre Chardonnay—the best she could find under the circumstances—a tub of butter, plastic bags of cheese and thinly sliced deli ham, half a dozen eggs, three apples, and a carton of half-n-half. Not much, but she'd only be there until Monday—three days. She opened the freezer.

The top freezer was empty, save for two ice cube trays. She dumped out the old ice, rinsed and refilled the trays, replaced them and stared into the icy, barren void. The state of the fridge and freezer bothered her—had Grandma been hard up and not said anything? She'd have sent Grandma money, had she known. *You'd send money, but not come visit.* Was that how she justified not visiting? Paying Grandma's bills a substitute to assuage her guilt? *I meant to come,* she lied to herself, knew she was lying to herself. *So, why didn't you?*

A rustling in the wall interrupted her self-analysis, drew her attention to the far side of the kitchen. She crossed the kitchen, opened the pantry door, stepped inside. The stench of mice and the scurry of tiny clawed paws across the plain wood shelves filled the space. She fumbled in the dark searching for the light cord, found it, and yanked it, catching a glimpse of little brown blurs in her peripheral vision.

Canned goods—some store bought tins, some glass home-canned jars—lined the shelves. The mice had shredded the boxes of dry goods, the corners nibbled away, had torn into bags of dried beans, the shelves littered with bits of cardboard, plastic, beans, and mouse shit. In the corner of the pantry, the chest freezer hummed. She opened it. Several cuts of meat—rump roast, pork loin, hamburger—all wrapped in white butcher paper and labeled with black marker. Plastic freezer bags, each holding two chicken leg quarters, no doubt originally from a ten-pound bag and divided. Bags of frozen vegetables furred in layers of fine ice. Frost grew from the sides of the freezer like mini icebergs.

She turned off the light and stepped back into the kitchen. At least Grandma hadn't been on the verge of starvation. *Does that make you feel better?*

"Fuck off," she muttered, closing the door. Weariness overtook her, her head swam, her limbs trembled and twitched from fatigue and hunger. She drank a glass of water and ate a slice of cheese, then left the kitchen.

She dragged her carry-on upstairs. Before heading to the bedroom she'd always stayed in as a child—it had been her father's—she stopped at the hallway linen closet and grabbed sheets, the sheets sun-bleached and soft from years of use. At the bedroom door, she hesitated a moment, then went in.

The bedroom seemed smaller than she remembered but otherwise the same: twin-sized bed shoved up in the corner against the wall, pressboard desk with a gooseneck lamp and metal chair, dresser with a mirror, short bookcase with old textbooks and a few paperbacks, Ole Miss pennants pinned on the walls, their colors faded. On the back of the closet door hung a men's short, navy blue, heavy cotton bathrobe—had that always been there?

She parked her carry-on beside the desk, changed the sheets, leaving the others in a pile on the floor, and switched on the window A/C unit, surprised but thankful it still worked, even if it tainted the air with a faint odor of mildew. She flipped off the overhead light, the moonlight streaming in through the dirty window guiding her to the bed, stripped off her clothes, and lay down on the fresh sheets.

III

IN THE EARLY HOURS BEFORE DAWN, Penny finally slipped into a deep, dreamless sleep, swallowed up in the cavernous void where the nightmares couldn't reach. In this space she hung, suspended, where time stopped, a minute stretching into eternity, eternity passing in a moment, until, at the distant edge of the void, a roar erupted, shattering the delicate shell of slumber, yanking her awake.

Panic and confusion crashed over her, the room unfamiliar until the wallpaper's floral pattern, yellow and faded with age, came into focus. Weak, early morning light strained through the dust-streaked windows, coating the room in a gray haze. Outside, a lawn mower passed, the roar growing louder as it moved along the side of the house, then fading as it went by. She checked the time. Just past 6:00 AM.

She snatched the bathrobe, tearing the hanging loop, and wrapped the robe around herself, tying the belt as she flew down the stairs, through the living room, the parlor, and out of the house. On the front porch, she stood and waited for the person mowing the lawn to come back around. The morning air, heavy and humid, groped at her and clung to her skin, the nape of her neck damp and clammy. A bead of perspiration rolled down her spine and seeped into her crack. The roar of the mower grew louder as it approached and rounded the corner.

The machine and the man pushing it came into view. He was shirtless, his t-shirt hanging from the back pocket of his faded, grass-stained jeans, his upper body slick and shiny with sweat, a red bandana tied around his head kept his long, unkempt hair out of his eyes. A cigarette dangled from the corner of his mouth. She yelled and waved her arms until she got his attention.

He stopped in front of the house, shut off the mower, gas and oil fumes mingled with the muggy air, and he grabbed the t-shirt, using it to wipe the back of his neck before addressing her. "Ma'am?"

"What the hell are you doing?" She crossed her arms over her chest. "Don't you know what time it is?"

He took the cigarette out of his mouth, turned his head and spat, and then squinted up at the sky as he spoke. "Mowin'. First job of the day." He looked toward her then, and after a moment, his eyes brightened. "Penny?"

"Yes?"

He sauntered up the porch stairs, stood two feet away from her. "You don't recognize me, do'ya?" He grinned, a lopsided grin, the left side of his mouth rising higher than the right.

Decades of cigarettes, sunlight, and hard-living masked the face of the boy she'd once known, but underneath he was there: the mismatched eyes—one brown, one hazel—the high cheekbones, the right side of his mouth that didn't work as well due to a brutal beating from his daddy long ago.

She peered closer at him. "Duncan?"

"Yeah," he said, moving in to hug her. When she side-stepped to avoid his embrace, he stepped back. "Oh, sorry. Forgot I was all sweaty."

She folded her arms tighter across her chest, uncomfortably aware she only wore a bathrobe. "Why are you here?"

"Mowin', like I tol' you." He leaned against one of the posts, casually smoking as if he had all the time in the world.

The flippant reply sparked a deep-seated fury, one she kept contained but still lay within her, smoldering.

"Asshole," she snapped. "You know what I mean."

Another grin. "Always mow for your granny once a week."

"In case you haven't noticed, she died six months ago."

"Church pays me to keep it up. Least 'til your family decides what to do with the property. Grass gets too high, it'll attract copperheads." He pulled a pack of cigarettes from his back pocket, shook one out, lit it off the tip of the last cigarette, and dropped the butt onto the porch, crushing it under his heel. "I can come back later this evenin' and finish up."

She turned toward the screen door. "You might as well finish now."

"Y'know, your granny used to fix me breakfast after I finished mowin.'"

"I'm not 'fixing' you breakfast."

"How's about some coffee?"

She didn't answer but went inside, letting the screen door bang shut behind her.

Duncan straightened up and started down the stairs. "I suppose I should tell folks to put up their dogs."

She shoved the screen door open. "What did you say?"

"Cream 'n sugar," he called over his shoulder, grinning, "Heavy on the sugar."

Back inside, she went upstairs, stripped off the robe, and took a long shower, scrubbing herself over and over until the hot water ran out, and then stood under the spray, letting the cold water chill her skin as she studied a cracked bubblegum pink tile. She shut off the water, stepped out and dried off, staring at the wallpaper, a dated pattern of palm fronds and flamingos, a riot of greens and pinks, several of the panels peeling at the top edges.

She let the damp towel drop to the floor and padded down the hall to the bedroom and lay back down on the bed, naked, closing her eyes, hoping to doze off but knowing she wouldn't. The window A/C unit blew at full blast but did little to dampen the noise of the mower as it circled the house like a hornet buzzing around its nest, droning on and on, getting closer with each circuit. The sound raked her skin, set her teeth on edge, and she abandoned any hope of sleep, got up, threw on a pair of jeans and a tank top, and headed back downstairs.

She made coffee, not because he'd asked for some, but because she wanted iced coffee. When the pot finished brewing, she filled a mug, doctored it with cream and sugar, and poured it into an ice-filled glass. Outside, the mowing had stopped and a peek out the kitchen window revealed Duncan loading the push mower into the back of a pick-up truck that had seen better days. As if sensing her gaze, he glanced over his shoulder at the house, nodding in her direction.

A strong urge to flip him off came over her, but she resisted, stepping back and letting the window sheers fall into place. *No reason to be a bitch. You're not a child. Be civil. Be polite. Make him a cup of coffee and send him on his merry-fucking way.* She poured another mug, the coffee strong with a hint of chicory, added two heaping spoons full of sugar and plenty of cream, stirring until it all melded together into a light tan. A thin layer of fat shimmered on the surface. With her glass in one hand and the mug in the other, she headed out to the front porch, pushing the screen door open with her hip, where Duncan waited, sitting on the metal porch glider, idly moving it back and forth. He'd put his t-shirt back on.

"Here." She handed him the coffee and went to sit on one of the peacock-backed rattan chairs, but time and weather had rotted out the seats of both chairs, so she settled at the other end of the glider.

"Thanks." He took a healthy slurp, wincing a bit when the hot liquid hit his tongue. He glanced at her. "You ain't havin' none?"

She lifted her glass. "Iced coffee."

The scent of fresh cut grass hung in the air. They sat and sipped their coffee in silence, Duncan with one leg stretched out, balanced on the heel of his work boot, bending and flexing his foot, gently moving the glider forward and back, the ice cubes in her glass tapping against the sides in time with the motion, the air thick and still, growing more oppressive as the minutes of the morning ticked by.

Duncan stirred, reached into his t-shirt pocket, pulled out his cigarettes. "Y'know, in hot places, like tropical places, they drink hot stuff to cool down." He offered her a cigarette, shrugged when she refused, and lit one up for himself. "If your insides are hot, makes your skin feel cool."

June bugs hovered inches above the ground. Long grass fringed the edges of the walkway leading up to the porch stairs, its concrete cracked and buckled by the oak tree roots. Weeds rimmed the base of the tree trunk. "Are you going to trim?" she asked.

"Ran out of gas. I'll come back later this evenin' 'n finish up." He drained his coffee.

She got up, held out her hand to take the empty mug. "Don't bother."

Picking up on her cue, he stood and handed it to her. "How long you plan on bein' here?"

"Not long." She opened the screen door. "Just until I get Grandma's things packed up."

"Need any help?"

She hesitated in the doorway. "No."

He ambled over to the top of the porch steps, still facing her, and leaned against the railing, his hand in his pocket, thumb hitched in a belt loop. "Y'wanna go get some breakfast?"

"No." She went inside.

Duncan watched her back receding into the darkness of the house before turning and going down the stairs. "Thanks for the coffee," he hollered and headed for his truck.

In the kitchen, she stood in front of the sink, pulled the sheers just enough to peek out the window at Duncan as he climbed into his pick-up truck and drove off. Written along the length of the truck bed was a slogan *Duncan CAN!* and a phone number, the paint chipped in places. On the fridge, among the fruit-shaped magnets holding small photos, newspaper clippings, and inspirational verses, was a business card with the same slogan and number, the corner of the cardstock smudged with an oily thumbprint.

The ice cubes in her drink had melted, leaving a watery, unpalatable mix. She dumped her drink, grabbed a clean mug, and poured herself a fresh cup of coffee, opting to drink it hot. She glanced at the clock above the kitchen doorway, but it was stuck at 4:45, so she checked her watch.

Before leaving Seattle, she'd arranged for the local Goodwill to come and take Grandma's furniture. The Goodwill people were supposed to arrive 'before noon,' and she debated with herself—was it worth starting to clear out one of the bedrooms and possibly miss them? She doubted she'd hear anything over the A/C units. *Or maybe you're procrastinating?* No, that wasn't it...was it? Convincing herself that she wasn't, in fact, procrastinating, she sat at the kitchen table, an old Formica top, a remnant from the '60s, its swirled aqua-green surface chipped at the corners and covered with cigarette burns from when her grandfather, a careless heavy smoker, had still been alive. Her briefcase lay on the table and from it she pulled out the blue-line copy of her manuscript and a mechanical pencil and started to go over the edits. She poured over the pages, line upon line, between sips of coffee, finishing one cup, and then another. The coffeepot, an older model, didn't have an automatic shut-off, and the remaining coffee slowly evaporated, concentrating, becoming stronger and more bitter as the morning wore on.

She drained the last of the coffee into her mug, added cream and sugar, the liquid turning a dull brown-gray, shut off the coffeepot, and sat back down to continue her work while she waited. A time check showed she still had a couple hours 'before noon'—whatever that meant.

She sipped her coffee, winced at the bitterness, and set the cup down, stretched, and tried to focus on the page in front of her. The blue words blurred, her eyes burned, and a nebulous headache formed behind her sockets. She set the pencil aside, hunched over, rested her head on her folded arms, and closed her eyes, just for a moment.

IV

SHARP, RAPID KNOCKING WOKE HER. "Hello?" *rapraprap* "Hello?"

Head still on her arms, she opened her eyes, stunned, discombobulated—why was she asleep at her desk, why was her secretary making such a damn racket? Or, had she fallen asleep during a session, prompting the patient to react in such a way? Her watch dug into her cheek, and she raised her head, a curse and an apology ready on her lips.

A metal-framed, vinyl-backed chair, white wisps of stuffing protruding from a crack in the fabric and avocado-green wallpaper patterned with free-floating mushrooms, asparagus stalks, potatoes, bundles of carrots and onions, came into focus as her eyes adjusted and she remembered where she was. The knocking continued.

rapraprap "Hello?!" *rapraprap* "Hello? Goodwill?!"

She checked the time. 11:45. Before noon.

She went to the front of the house and opened the screen door. "Sorry, I didn't hear you."

"Yes, ma'am. You scheduled a pick-up?" The man, in his mid-50s, his face as bland as a blank sheet of paper, dressed in the type of second-hand work coveralls found in a thrift store, consulted a small spiral notebook as he spoke. Behind him stood two younger men; one was blonde, fresh-faced with a smirk, the other was darker, hollowed-faced, shifting from foot to foot as if he couldn't be still.

She stepped aside, opening the door wider. "Come in."

"Thank you, ma'am," the older man said, entering, the other two following after him. The blonde, bold and cocky, winked as he passed her, the side of his neck red and patchy with the faint outlines of an old tattoo just below the surface of the skin. The darker man simply nodded, avoided looking at her directly.

After explaining what she wanted taken away—all of the furniture in the parlor and living room—she headed back to the kitchen with plans to continue going over the edits but stared at the wall instead, listening to the ambient conversations of the men without really hearing what they said, lost in the benign pattern of the wallpaper while vague memories, diaphanous like ghosts, floated and flitted in and out of her mind, images and apparitions of Grandma hustling about the kitchen, biscuits and red-eye gravy.

In true Southern hospitality, Grandma would've made a fresh pot of coffee for the men. Out of a mixture of nostalgia and guilt, she got up and went through the motions of making coffee. While the pot brewed, she gathered clean mugs and spoons, took the half-n-half out of the fridge, searched for the sugar bowl to no avail, having to settle for setting out the sugar container instead, and arranged all the items on the counter, then waited and watched the liquid fill the carafe until it gurgled and sputtered out the last drop.

She stood in the kitchen doorway. The men had made significant progress clearing out the furniture, leaving behind dust bunnies as big as rabbits. The older man held the screen door open as the two younger men maneuvered one of the nicer parlor couches out of the house. Bluebottle flies swarmed inside. Once the young men were out the door, the older man grabbed two lamps and followed out after them.

When the three reentered the house, she called out, "Would you gentlemen like some coffee?"

The older man, red-faced and panting, pulled a handkerchief out of his back pocket and wiped his face. "Yes, ma'am, that'd be appreciated."

"Come help yourselves," she said, turning away and back into the kitchen. Perhaps a cold drink would've been more appropriate, though all she had to offer was chilled Chardonnay. She made herself a fresh cup before stepping aside to let the men make their own. "Or, help yourselves to water, if you prefer," she offered. "There's ice in the freezer. Glasses in that cabinet."

'Coffee's fine' was the collective reply. The older man took his black. The bold blonde, still smirking, took creamer. The dark twitchy one added creamer and several heaping teaspoons of sugar to his, cradled the mug with both hands, lifting it to his lips, taking a long, savoring sip. He smiled and nodded at her.

The men didn't speak, not to each other or to her, and she didn't feel compelled to offer any small talk. When he had finished, the older man rinsed his mug and placed it in the sink. He cleared his throat. "Ma'am, what do you want to do with that short bookcase in the parlor?"

"Take it with the rest of the stuff."

"Well, ma'am, there's still books on it."

His insistence on calling her 'ma'am' grated on her nerves for reasons she couldn't pinpoint. "So, take the books too. I don't care."

"They ain't boxed up, ma'am."

Did he know he irritated her? "Oh for Chr—"

"I take them." The dark man had spoken, his accent one she couldn't place—Eastern European, maybe? "If you have box, I take them." He paused, shifted his eyes toward the older man. "If is okay, Mr. Lowry?"

Mr. Lowry rubbed the back of his neck, sighing with resignation. "If she's willin' to give'm to you. And if we got room in the truck."

She graced the dark man with a smile. "You're welcome to them."

She followed the men back to the parlor, pointing to the boxes she'd left there, telling the dark man to help himself.

"I may take all books?" he asked, his eyes wide, wonder painted across his features.

"Yes, please do."

"Thank you, Miss." He gave a small bow of his head. "Thank you."

He knelt, as if in prayer, in front of the bookcase, removed a book, reverently, wiping dust from its spine with his sleeve, cradling the book in one hand while smoothing his fingers across the cover, his lips moving as he silently read the title before lowering it into the box, repeating the ritual with the next book he removed. The other two men moved coffee tables out of the house. She retreated back to the kitchen. She'd planned to wait until the men left before getting a glass of wine, but her nerves were raw, jagged, exposed, the air like fire on her skin. *To hell with it.* She grabbed a bottle out of the fridge and a glass tumbler from the cabinet.

With a tumbler of wine, she sat at the table, attempted to continue reviewing the edits, but after a few moments, her eyes drifted from the page, settled on the opposite wall, mindlessly studying the wallpaper, wandering aimlessly in a forest of memories.

A tap on the doorjamb roused her back to the present. The dark man hesitated in the doorway. "Miss?"

She acknowledged his presence with a glance, and he approached, carrying two books.

"These," he said, laying the books before her like an offering, "these you should keep."

Before she had the chance to speak, to tell him to just take them, Mr. Lowry stepped into the room. "Omar," he said with a jerk of his head, "let's go."

"Yes, Mr. Lowry," Omar said. Before leaving, he bowed slightly to her. "Thank you, Miss." He pointed at the books. "Special. You should keep." He smiled and left the kitchen.

Mr. Lowry directed his attention to her, placing a sheet of paper over the books. "Ma'am, here's a form you can fill out. For tax purposes." He leaned forward, pointing at the bottom of the page. "I've already signed it. You just hav'ta list what you've donated and the estimated value."

"Thank you," she said. She had no intention of filling out the form.

She felt obligated to show him out, something her grandma would've done, though Grandma would've continued to thank him as they walked through the house. She had no intention of doing that either.

In the living room, she stopped. Her grandfather's recliner remained the only piece of furniture left in the room. "Wait. That goes too."

Mr. Lowry paused and turned toward her. "Well, ma'am. We had another pick-up earlier, and there's no more room in the truck."

"Are you coming back to get it?"

"Sorry, ma'am, we ain't like a moving company. We gotta unload the truck, then we're scheduled for another pick-up."

An image flashed, temporarily blinding her—a knife in her hand, covered in blood, Mr. Lowry twitching on the floor, his mouth gapping, his eyes bugging as he bled out. She closed her eyes, took a deep breath before speaking, "Can you come back tomorrow?"

"Morrow's Saturday?" He consulted his battered notebook. "We're full up for Saturday." He licked his finger and flipped a page. "Earliest we could come back is sometime Monday. Maybe before noon."

She said this was fine, she'd have more furniture for them to take by then. She followed him to the front door. "Do I have to be here?"

"Well, somebody needs to be." He paused. "Don't have to be you, ma'am."

She bit her tongue to keep from cursing and made a mental note to call Grandma's lawyer, make him come on Monday to wait for the Goodwill truck to show up.

The men left, pulling away in the truck. Omar sat in the seat next to the window, a box of books balanced on his knees, and gave a small wave as they drove off. She didn't wave back but turned away, strode through the parlor, the living room, ignored the recliner sitting solitary in the open space, her footsteps loud in the empty rooms, retreated into the kitchen, heading straight for the fridge and refreshed her wine, adding a few ice cubes to the tumbler. For several minutes, she leaned back against the counter and stared at the books on the table. The top one she recognized at once—her grandmother's Bible.

Condensation collected on her glass, the swollen beads too heavy to cling to the slick surface pooled and dripped from her fingers. *Stop procrastinating. You've got to start packing stuff.* Instead, she tore off a paper towel, folded it into quarters, sat down, and pulled the black tome in front of her.

She opened the Bible. It had originally belonged to her great-grandmother, a woman she'd never met, though vague memories of Grandma's stories about the matriarch filtered through Penny's mind—something about her great-grandmother being a missionary 'to the heathen' before marrying her husband.

A family tree sprawled across the inside of the cover, thick and dense, like an ancient oak growing in the dark heart of a forest. Started by her great-grandmother, Grandma had continued to meticulously record births and deaths, marriages, divorces, remarriages, adding branches and twigs, for she'd had six siblings, Penny's great-grandparents having taken the commandment to 'go forth and multiply' seriously, and while Grandma had been their oldest child, she'd outlived all of her brothers and sisters. The handwriting served as a record of her grandma's advancing age, early entries written in a firm, neat hand, eventually, gradually evolving to the light, spidery scrawl Penny recognized best.

The pages were tissue thin, the edges soft and foxed from age and use, passages underlined, notes scribbled in the margins—her grandma's doing. Every few pages she found some church bulletin, leaflet, or scrap of paper tucked inside. Her high school graduation invitation was there, stuck in the latter half of Genesis—it'd been one of the few times Grandma had traveled away from the state to visit, had insisted on coming by bus. Between the last page and the back cover were several envelopes containing old letters, names and addresses Penny didn't recognize, probably great-aunts and uncles she'd never met. One envelope stood out from the rest. It was sealed. She turned it over. Her name was written across the front. Perhaps it was an extra copy of Grandma's Will, but the contents felt too thin, too light, the envelope plain and common.

The harsh, jangly ring of Grandma's telephone cut through Penny's curiosity, caused her to jump at the sudden intrusion of noise. She glared at the phone, an AT&T Bell relic in a dingy avocado green, the edges browned from age and oxidation, and she willed it to stop ringing. It didn't—and Grandma had never owned an answering machine. Cursing under her breath, she crammed the unopened envelope and the rest of the letters back into the Bible, shoved it to the side, got up, and answered the phone with a brusque, "Yes."

The caller on the other end seemed momentarily stunned, taking several beats to reply. "Is this Ms. Penny?"

Dear God. The man's voice, light, soft, slightly effeminate, was familiar. *The fucking preacher.* "Yes," she repeated.

A few more beats of silence, as if he were trying to process her response. "This is Pastor Jones. How are you today?"

It was her turn to be quiet, to breathe deeply, to control her tongue. "I'm well. How can I help you?" She tried to pace the floor, but the phone cord only stretched as far as the stove, and she wondered what Grandma had done with the cordless phone she'd sent years ago.

"I heard you were in town, getting Sister Connie's house in order, so to speak, and we were wondering if you needed any help?"

Damn you, Duncan. With all the politeness she could muster, she assured Pastor Jones she was fine, didn't need any help, thanked him for the offer.

But he was a difficult man to get off the phone. After listening to him praising the memory of her grandma and enduring no less than three invitations to Sunday service, he finally took a breath long enough for her to say 'goodbye' and hang up the phone. She picked up her glass, only to discover she'd polished off her drink while on the phone, and poured herself another, told herself she needed to start packing but sat down instead, grabbing the second book.

Except, it wasn't a book but a photo album, the photographs held in place with corner holders, dates and events written under each snapshot. She was prominent in the photos, some taken there at her grandparents' home, others her mother had sent, school pictures ranging from kindergarten through her doctorate, photos from Christmases, birthdays, Easters, Halloweens.

At some images, she lingered: the Halloween when she was four and dressed up as Little Red Riding Hood, leading the family German Shepard by leash in one hand, basket in the other. She eased the photo from its place, studied it closer, a small smile played across her lips as she gazed at her younger self, her blonde hair plaited into two pigtails, a white cotton shirt with ruffles at the wrists, a forest green, mid-calf length full skirt with straps that came over her shoulders and attached to the skirt waist with leather-covered buttons, the picoted edge of a petticoat peeking out beneath the hem, and a dark crimson hooded cape that reached almost to her ankles, as if she'd stepped out of a fairy tale. How she had loved that costume. Grandma had made it, sewn from good fabric made to last, and had mailed it off to Virginia in time for Halloween.

A photo from the first summer she'd spent at her grandparents' house by herself. She'd been six. She and Duncan splashed in a kiddie pool, naked, smooth-skinned and flat-chested, brown from the summer sun, Duncan's hair nearly as long as hers, the sun catching the reddish highlights in his dark hair, his skin the color of coffee and cream, her own skin not as dark, remnants of a sunburn glowed across her nose and cheeks, her hair sun-bleached to the color of corn silk. Out of the picture frame, someone—her grandfather—sprayed them with the garden hose, their mouths fixed in squeals, their innocent bodies glistening.

More photos from that first summer: Penny helping her grandmother in the garden. Another one of her with an exaggerated smile, showing off a missing front tooth, faint traces of tears smeared across her face. Her and Duncan sitting at the picnic table, both of them shirtless, eating watermelon, juice and seeds dripping down their chests and forearms. She flipped through more photos recording her first summer away from home.

She paused at the last of those images. It'd been taken in the living room, most likely by her father, before her parents took her back home to Richmond; a photo of her, Grandma, and her grandfather, composed around his recliner. Grandma stood to the side, slightly behind the recliner, her hand gripping the back, her smile seemed pained, as if it took effort. Her grandfather sat upright in the chair, beamed a wide toothy grin, Penny on his lap, his huge hand with his long, thick fingers wrapped around her middle. Penny wore a red gingham sundress Grandma had made for her during that visit—she'd let Penny pick the fabric out herself—and dainty white sandals bought at Franklin's, especially for church. Penny didn't smile as she sat on her grandfather's lap.

It was the last photo he'd be in. He'd be found dead, two days later, in his recliner.

She slammed the photo album shut, shoved her chair away from the table; the swift, violent movement toppled over the salt and pepper shakers and sent the table back several inches, the metal legs screeching against the linoleum. She snatched several trash bags from the box, pinning them under her arm, and grabbed the wine out of the fridge. With the bottle in one hand and her glass in the other, she left the kitchen, dashed through the living room, and headed upstairs.

V

She'd been upstairs for hours, underestimating how long it'd take to clear out her grandparents' bedrooms. Separate bedrooms—how odd, something she'd never noticed as a child when her family spent a week of her father's vacation there every year, nor the first summer she'd spent there on her own. Her grandfather had always seemed to fall asleep in his recliner. Of course, children don't really notice such things. Grandma had been an 'early to bed, early to rise' woman, so perhaps that explained it.

Grandma hadn't thrown away any of Grandfather's things, even though he'd been dead for decades, and when Penny had entered his bedroom, it seemed as if Grandma hadn't even gone into the room since his death, and it felt like opening a mausoleum.

It didn't take long to fill up the trash bags she'd brought up, and she had to go downstairs for more. She brought up the whole box. Clothes—pants, shirts, a suit, jackets, underwear, socks—were balled up and shoved into bags, along with shoes and boots, destined to be thrown away. At the very back of her grandfather's chifforobe, hidden under a stack of dress shirts, were magazines, magazines Grandma surely hadn't known about, the glossy pages dulled by time and humidity. Penny didn't bother flipping through them, just crammed them into one of the bags. An assortment of toiletries—cans, tubes, bottles, boxes—covered the surface of his bureau, the items caked in dust, the dust so dense it'd collected into gray chunks among the items, like looking down upon a miniature replica of a ruined city. She cleared off the bureau, swiping everything into the bag with her hand. The dust, thick and tacky from age, oils, and humidity, clung to her, and she rubbed her hand down the length of her thigh to get it off. The dust came off, stuck to her jeans like a gray fungus, but the greasy residue remained on her skin.

After dealing with the chifforobe and bureau, she stripped the linens off the bed, the mattress underneath sweat-stained; she couldn't imagine anyone being desperate enough to want it, but that was for the thrift shop to decide. Not her problem.

Grandma's room took more time. As Penny removed the clothes from their hangers, she folded each item before placing it in a bag. She sat on the side of the bed and went through the nightstand drawer. Several religious books, more than a year's worth of *Daily Guideposts*, a notebook, a few pens, all of which went into a bag. Next, she sorted through the chest dresser, separating items to donate and items to throw away. In the back of one of the top drawers were bundles of letters held together by rubber bands. Penny's handwriting spread across the envelopes, progressing from childish blocky misshapen letters to preteen loopy cursive with hearts dotting the i's.

She went to throw away the bundles but paused, sat on the edge of the bed, and undid the rubber band from one of the bundles. The band, brittle and tacky, broke apart as she pulled it off, leaving bits of rubber stuck to the envelope. Many of the letters were thank-you notes; her father had been an only child, she the only grandchild, and Grandma had often sent small packages to her, books, candy, stuffed animals, little trinkets picked up at the 5 & 10. She read through a few of the letters, then set them aside, unsure whether she wanted to keep them or not. Something, like an ache, squeezed her heart, a longing for a simpler time—perhaps, to be a child again. *Childhood is never simple.* A rush of rage, inexplicable and senseless, seized her, and she grabbed all of the letters, shoved them in a bag, and pushed herself off the bed. She needed to press on.

VI

WEARINESS HUNG OVER HER, weighing down her shoulders, her neck and back achy from the strain of bending, stooping, and lifting all afternoon. She'd lost count of the number of trips up and down the stairs, lugging the heavy bags, separating them: bags for donations placed in the parlor, bags destined for the trash stacked on and around the recliner. By the time she'd finished, the sun had dipped low into the horizon but withheld none of its heat.

After dropping the last garbage bag beside the recliner, she went into the kitchen and washed the grime off her hands before pouring herself more wine and making a sandwich. She leaned back against the counter as she ate, debating which part of the house to tackle next. But in that moment, just taking a bite of sandwich, chewing and swallowing, took effort; she forced herself to eat.

Her tank top and jeans were stiff. She'd sweated through them several times, despite the upstairs A/C window units being cranked up to the highest setting. Fine layers of salt and grit coated her skin. With the last bite of sandwich, she made a decision: a shower first and then she'd decide what to do next.

Upstairs, in the bathroom, she adjusted the water to be as hot as she could stand before flipping on the showerhead and stepping under the spray. She washed her hair, added conditioner, scrubbed her body over and over until the hot water ran out, rinsing her hair in the cool water. It struck her that the only times she'd taken two showers in one day was when she had a lover. A smile, as brief as a burst of sunlight on an overcast day, sprang to her face only to fade away as quickly as it had appeared.

The shower didn't perk her up or renew her resolve, and as she toweled off, the last bit of energy seeped out of her. Through the small window above the showerhead, dusk had descended, and in the treetops, the evening's first lightning bugs flashed secret signals to each other. As a child, she'd complain when she had to go to bed in the summer when it was still light enough outside to play, but now all she wanted was to sleep. But, going to bed so early meant she risked waking up in the middle of the night, lying in the dark, battling the demons that only came at 2:00 AM when sleep was elusive.

She padded down the hallway to the bedroom, clutching the towel around her body. In the bedroom, she draped the towel over the back of the desk chair and cranked the A/C unit as high as it would go. From her carry-on, she dug out a bottle of prescription sleeping pills, having thrown them in at the last minute when she'd packed. She hated taking sleeping pills, loathed surrendering control, and reserved them for only when absolutely necessary, but the prospect of a full night's sleep was too tempting. She shook a pill out into her palm.

On the nightstand sat her glass with a few swallows of wine left, and, doing what she warned her patients never to do, she popped the pill on her tongue and washed it down with the remainder of the wine. She switched off the bedside lamp and then stretched out, naked, on the bed, not bothering to get under the sheets. In her head, she heard Grandma's admonishment: nice girls wore pajamas to bed. Penny grinned at the paradox. Children skinny-dipping was fine, but sleeping naked was not.

The early evening dim muted the room to a washed-out grayish-blue. The A/C hummed. A tree frog chirped near the window. She closed her eyes, waited for sleep to pull her down into its depths. She sensed it, just out of reach, stalking her like a wolf hunting a hare in a dark forest, creeping closer and closer until it sprung upon her, and she surrendered, allowing herself to sink; the sounds of the A/C and the frog grew fainter, and beyond, the buzzing of hornets.

VII

Duncan pulled into the driveway, the gravel crunching under the truck wheels, parked, and shut off the ignition. He lit a cigarette, listening to the engine *tick* as it cooled. In the early evening dim, tree frogs chirped, and fireflies blinked in the trees.

He got out, pulled off his t-shirt and hung it in the open window. As he walked around the truck bed, he glanced over at the house. Lights were on upstairs. Maybe after he'd finished trimming the yard, he'd see if Penny wanted to grab a beer, catch up. Probably not, but it didn't hurt none to ask.

He started up the weed trimmer and went about his work. The muggy air clung to him, the damp mingled with his sweat until his skin was slick, beaded up until the sweat ran down his back, his arms, dripped from the tip of his nose, as he made a circuit around the yard, trimming the perimeter before moving to the trees in the backyard and the shed, then around the base of the house, finishing up with the oak tree in the front.

After putting the weed trimmer back in the truck bed, he took off his bandana and wiped the sweat, grime, and bits of grass from his face. He swiped the cloth under his armpits for good measure and slipped on his t-shirt. He hunched down to check his appearance in the wing mirror, combed his fingers through his hair, his hair shaggy with streaks of gray, his scalp damp with sweat. *Good enough.*

He sauntered across the yard, up the front porch steps, and knocked on the door. Waited. Knocked again. The downstairs lights were off—

maybe she was still upstairs. He opened the door—nobody locked their doors in Osyka—and stepped inside, closing the door behind him.

"Penny?" His voice echoed off the walls. The parlor was dark, the shades drawn down, blocking any residual light. The room felt empty. He stepped in farther, his foot knocking against something on the floor, and he flipped the light switch. All of the parlor furniture had been removed. Garbage bags lined the wall. He moved through the living room, empty except for the old man's recliner and more garbage bags piled on and around it, and into the kitchen.

He checked the fridge, hoping to find a beer. No beer, just wine. Penny's granny hadn't been a drinker, but she'd always kept a few beers in the fridge for him. He'd never known his grandparents, and the old woman didn't have a grandson and her son had lived far away, too far to do for her like a son should, so she and Duncan had sort of adopted each other. Hell, growing up, Granny had fed him more often than his own mama had. He wasn't ashamed to admit that at Granny's funeral he'd sat in the back pew and bawled like a baby.

He helped himself to a glass of water, not bothering with ice, and gulped it down quick. He refilled the glass, leaned back against the counter and sipped it, randomly glancing around the kitchen. Last time he'd stepped foot in the house had been at the wake when the table and countertops were laden with food, and everyone had waited for Penny to show up, but after an hour, it had become apparent she wasn't going to show, and everyone had gone ahead and dug in, had spent the afternoon eating and sharing memories about Granny, or Sister Connie, as most of the folks had referred to her.

Now the kitchen, a space as familiar to him as his own home, seemed off, somehow strange. The clock above the kitchen doorway said 4:45, which wasn't right, its hands frozen in place.

A lone cast iron skillet sat on the back burner of the stove, its surface black with a hard shine, well-seasoned, never had a drop of soap touched it. Granny could cook a three-course meal with that skillet, and suddenly he had a taste in his mouth for fried pork chops and country gravy, thick and white and full of black pepper. A ceramic shaker with "Love" written on it sat on the back of the stove. It'd been there for as long as he could remember.

On the opposite wall hung a copy of a painting—an old man sitting at a table, his head bowed in prayer over a plate of bread, the colors dark and solemn—on either side of the print hung a pair of huge utensils—a fork and a spoon, each a yard long, carved from wood and lacquered. A small lopsided grin ticked the good corner of his mouth—how old had he been when he made those in shop class? Fifteen? A gift for Granny. He finished his drink and set the glass in the sink. The items on the table had caught his eye.

He approached the briefcase in a roundabout way, trailing his hand across the scratched and cigarette-burn-pocked tabletop, feeling the grit of stray salt grains, until his hand brushed against the side of the briefcase and he allowed his hand to venture farther. He touched the surface, first smoothing his palm over it, then stroking it with his fingertips, the leather soft and supple, slightly yielding to his touch, and it felt like sparks traveled up his fingertips, through his fingers, spread through his hand, and made it warm. The briefcase laid on its back, open, the flap buckle resting on the table. He peeked inside—just a bunch of long-ass papers with blue print and some handwriting, done in pencil, scrawled on the margins.

The leather binding of Granny's Bible wasn't nearly as fine as the briefcase. The Bible's binding showed decades of daily use, flecks of black coating missing, revealing the thin, cheap leather underneath, the gold lettering 'HOLY BIBLE' nearly rubbed off, the edges of the cover cracked and torn. He opened it, though it felt like sacrilege to do so, like entering the Holy of Holies unwashed. A family tree sprawled across the inside covers, thick and dense with limbs, branches, twigs, some of the writing so tiny even he couldn't read it, and he had good eyesight. He closed the book.

The last item turned out to be a photo album. He opened it. He liked looking at other folks' pictures, probably because he had so few of his own. Most of the photos were of Penny: school pictures, Penny sitting on the laps of mall Santas, Easters and frilly dresses, Halloween costumes. Several of the photos were from summers when she used to come stay with Granny, and he was in many of those. One where they were skinny-dipping in a kiddie pool, squealing as her Pappy squirted them with a garden hose. That'd been the first summer she stayed by herself, the summer he'd met her. He grinned as he turned the pages—memories, quick and vivid, rushing and flashing at him.

He paused a bit longer at one photo: he and Penny asleep on the back porch. She'd been seven, he'd've been nine in a few weeks. It'd been a rainy day, and they'd built a blanket fort on the screened-in back porch, had spent the day playing in it. She'd begged Granny to let him spend the night—they wanted to 'camp out'—and when Granny hadn't been able to get his mama on the phone, she'd reckoned it'd be okay. He and Penny were going to stay up all night but had fallen asleep—they'd argued the next day about who'd fallen asleep first; he'd claimed she fell asleep while he told a ghost story, she'd insisted she'd been faking to fool him—and at some point in the night, Granny had grabbed her camera and snapped a picture, the light from the kitchen falling across their faces, faces still young and smooth and pure.

The sudden ache in his soul surprised Duncan. He wasn't one to dwell much on the past, but for a brief moment, he mourned for that boy, the boy who was mischievous but still good, whose smile wasn't yet lopsided, who still believed he could be anything he wanted, even the President of the United States, or an astronaut, or rich—all those fairy tales fed to children. He had an urge to take the photo, as if stealing it might reverse time, but he resisted and turned the page.

More photos, like a time lapse, and Penny grew up before his eyes.

Where was she? All this time, he'd expected her to come downstairs, fuss at him for coming in the house, making himself at home, touching her stuff, looking at her things. He closed the photo album, stood still, and listened. Outside, the tree frogs continued their mating calls. Inside, the fridge hummed. From the pantry came a faint scurrying. Mice. Granny's cat had wandered off after she died, never returned. He strained to detect any movement upstairs, but the only human sound was his own breathing.

He left the kitchen, forgetting to turn off the light. It seemed awful early for a person to go to bed. As he passed the doorway that led upstairs, curiosity got the better of him. He stuck his head in the stairwell. "Penny?" he called, his voice low and husky like a stage whisper. "Penny? You up?"

No response. No movement.

He eased up the stairs, slow, cautious, stealthy, as if stalking a deer. He didn't want to spook her—she might have a baseball bat or a knife. Any woman could do some damage with a baseball bat if a man was caught off guard, and he already knew what she could do with a knife. She didn't seem like the type who'd own a gun.

At the top of the stairs, he paused. Only one of the bedroom doors were shut, the one at the end of the hallway, the one she'd stayed in as a girl. He crept toward the door, not making a sound, his breathing steady and even, his senses alert, listening for any hint of movement, but the only sound was the dull, muffled hum of the A/C unit inside the room.

When he reached the door, he pushed it open gently, little by little, until he could step inside.

On the twin-sized bed, curled up on her side, facing into the room, Penny slept on top of the sheets, naked, her hair splayed over the pillow, a blonde wisp across her cheek. Sleep softened her face, erased decades from her features, revealing the young girl he once knew, and he remembered again the sleepover and how he had watched her sleep, her lips then, as now, slightly parted as she breathed, her side gently rising and falling, and the memory stabbed him.

He moved closer. The moon shone through the tree outside the window, her thigh speckled in moonlight and shadow, and he wanted to reach out and touch her, smooth the palm of his hand over her dappled thigh, stroke it with his fingertips, feel her skin yield to his touch. For long moments, he fought this urge. A light summer blanket, folded, hung over the footboard, and he pulled it over her body, covering her.

He slipped out of the bedroom, eased the door closed behind him, pulling it until he heard the latch catch, and then made his way downstairs and out of the house, making sure to lock the front door behind him. Once in his truck, he didn't start the engine right away but sat and smoked a cigarette.

By the time he finished his cigarette, lit another one, and started up the truck, he'd decided to go to Jo-Jo's 24-Hour Diner for supper. He still had a hankering for fried pork chops, though he knew they wouldn't be nearly as good.

VIII

PENNY WOKE UP COLD; goosebumps covered her exposed skin, raising the fine hairs on her arms. Condensation dripped from the window unit, the air in the room cold and clammy like winter in Seattle. A thin summer blanket draped her body, though it provided no warmth, and she was strangely aware of her nakedness. She slept in the nude all the time, even during the coldest months in Seattle, slipping under layers of sheets, heavy blankets, and a down comforter, never giving it a second thought, but now she was hyperaware of her body, of the texture of the blanket against her skin, and she felt exposed, naughty, as if she were a child and had done something very bad, like being caught touching herself. She flung the blanket off, got out of bed, rummaged through her carry-on for clean clothes. Despite the years of yoga and Pilates, her breasts and belly showed the advancement of time, and as she dressed, she avoided her reflection in the mirror.

She wandered into the kitchen in the haze of a half-remembered dream, wisps of an image clouding her thoughts—wolves dressed as men riding giant toads, the toads flicking their long, thick, sticky tongues—only to dissipate into smoke when she tried to latch onto it. She didn't hold much stock in dream analysis, but she couldn't shake the feeling of vulnerability and shame that lingered. She took the coffee can from the cabinet and rationalized her feelings—a side effect from the sleeping pill, nothing more.

She measured out grounds for a full pot, slid the filter basket into place, and went to fill the carafe with water but paused. In the sink sat an empty glass. Had she gotten up during the night? She couldn't remember, residual fog clouded her mind, dulled her thoughts. She shook herself and filled the carafe.

A cup of coffee in one hand and the box of trash bags in the other—she'd have to get another box soon—she headed upstairs. It didn't take long to clear out the bathroom and the linen closet; everything left in the bathroom could be tossed, most of the linen items donated. In the very back of the linen closet, behind a stack of old towels, was the cordless phone she'd sent Grandma years ago, still in the box. *So, that's where it was.* Grandma had always been suspicious of 'contraptions,' and if the old things still worked, why replace them? The phone went into the donation bag.

She cleared out the desk, bookcase, closet, and dresser in her father's old bedroom. Grandma had saved several of Dad's things, mostly mementos from his school and college days, but she doubted her father would even remember any of it, and she used the last trash bag. Hauling the bags downstairs seemed to take more time than it did to fill them. Her muscles protested, still aching from the day before, and after setting the last bag next to the recliner—the bag tottered, threatening to fall over—she decided to take a brief break for a sandwich, eating from necessity rather than true hunger. With a fresh cup of coffee in hand, she went into the living room, set her cup on the mantlepiece among her grandma's knickknacks, and faced the door to the storage space under the stairs.

Grandma hadn't been a hoarder, one of those people often exploited on reality T.V. shows. Grandma's generation loathed to throw anything away, using things until they wore out or broke down beyond repair, and then, as the original upcyclers, they'd find other uses for these items if possible—old towels became cleaning rags, clothes were mended over and over again, handed down until they were threadbare, and then the good parts cut up and made into quilts, plastic shopping bags crocheted into placemats, grocery lists written on the backs of used envelopes, vegetable scraps and coffee grounds went into compost piles, and a Sunday ham would feed a family for over a week, the bone saved to add flavor to beans. That generation had had its own version of 'recycle, reduce, reuse,' and Penny wondered if the old ways had been better.

But, standing in front of the open storage space, the space packed tight with decades of stuff, she groaned. *This is going to take all damn day.* A spider dashed out of the space, and she jumped, yelped, chased it down across the dusty floor, and stomped on it.

Her grandma had been an organized woman, but as Penny began to pull a sundry of items and objects out of the storage space, there seemed to be no apparent rhyme or reason to what had been shoved in there. Perhaps Grandma had used the space the way others use a spare bedroom, stashing away things just to get them out of the way. Like an archeological dig, new layers gave way to older layers, and she spread her findings across the living room floor to be shifted through. More spiders ran out into the open. Silverfish, sheltering in piles of papers, surprised at being moved, streaked out and over her fingers. She pulled out a cushion, finely embroidered in an intricate floral pattern—she vaguely remembered the cushion as one of a pair which had graced each corner of the nicer parlor couch—its corner shredded, tufts of poly-fil poking out, no doubt the work of mice looking to line their nests. *Where's the other cushion?* She found its mate, the embroidery work snagged, the flowers distorted, the fabric puckered. Perhaps Grandma had meant to mend it but never got to do so. She tossed the cushions aside and continued her excavations.

As she set another stack of papers against the living room wall, there was a knock at the front door. She dropped the pile, sending the silverfish hidden inside scurrying. "Who the hell could that be?" she muttered, vaguely worried it might be Grandma's pastor.

Duncan stood on the porch, his thumbs hitched in his front pockets. Clean jeans, fresh t-shirt, his hair still damp from a shower, he smelled of soap and Old Spice.

"Mornin'." The lopsided grin appeared.

"I said not to bother with the weed trimming," she said but stepped back to let him in.

He closed the screen door behind him. "I came back and did it last night." He paused. "I suppose you was asleep."

She headed back into the living room. He followed, whistling at all the stuff strewn across the floor. She paused at the fireplace mantle, went to take a sip of the cold coffee but stopped—a fly floated on the surface.

"Damn flies," she said.

"Your granny was always sayin' she wanted to clear this out," he said, poking his head into the opened storage. "Tol' her to gimme a holler and I'd help her."

"What do you want?"

"Nothin'. Just came by, see how you was doin'. Damn, it's hot in here." He glanced up. "Why don't you have the ceiling fans runnin'?"

She wiped her forehead with the back of her hand. "They just stir the hot air around."

"Probably need to be reversed. You switch'em over in the summer."

Before she could speak, he retrieved a chair from the kitchen, stood on it, slid some button at the base of the fan, stepped down, and turned it on. Papers fluttered off some of the piles, and she grabbed several old shoes from the storage space to weigh the piles down. He went into the parlor and reversed the ceiling fan in there. The chair creaked as he stepped down and called out, "Now, you open the windows, keep the front and back doors open, and you get a cross breeze goin'. It'll cool it down some." From the parlor came the sound of windows being forced open, the humidity-swollen frames screeching in protest, the wood threatening to crack. In the living room, he opened the windows on either side of the fireplace then disappeared into the kitchen, opening windows and the back door. She heard him fiddling with something.

"Help yourself to coffee," she offered, then wondered why the hell she did so.

He came back, carrying two cups, and handed one to her.

"Oh. Thanks," she said.

They sipped their coffee in uncomfortable silence.

"The latch is broke on that back screen door. Got my toolbox in the truck. I'll fix it for you." He surveyed the room. The ceiling fans whined. "Probably wouldn't hurt to oil those fans. But, it does help, don't it?"

While the room wasn't cool by any stretch of the imagination, she did have to admit it did knock down the oppressive heat somewhat. A fly buzzed near her, and she swatted at it.

"Granny probably got some fly paper 'round here," he said. "Or, I can get you some."

"I'll find it." She placed her cup down beside the other one. "Did you want something?" She used her dismissive tone, the one she gave to her secretary when the woman was being particularly irritating. She hoped Duncan took the hint.

Instead, he bent over, set his cup on the hearth, and when he stood up, his demeanor had changed; he seemed shy, a bit sheepish, not meeting her eyes, a faint hint of color on his copper cheeks, like the beginnings of a sunburn. He reached into his back pocket and pulled something out.

"You remember this?" he asked as he offered it to her.

It was a sheet of pink construction paper folded into quarters, the color faded, the edges tinted brown from age. She undid the first fold, revealing a heart and flowers, drawn in crayon, the words GET WELL SOON written across the top in a child's uncertain print. She opened the card. Inside were more random crayon drawings—more hearts and flowers, a cat for some reason—and a note written on one half:

> I'm sorry your sick.
> I hope you feel bettr soon.
> Love.
> Penny

She'd misspelled "better" and had corrected it by printing a tiny 'e' in the space above the 't' and 'r'. How old had she been when she made the card? Seven? Maybe eight?

Penny, who prided herself on being able to pinpoint and analyze away her emotions, who had cast aside childish things, who had hermetically sealed off the part of her heart where childhood memories resided, was momentarily disarmed as memory and emotion welled up, threatened to overwhelm her, and as she stroked the waxy letters, her eyes stung.

She closed the card and handed it back to him, avoiding his eyes. "I sent this to Grandma to give to you. She'd said you were in the hospital, that you were sick." She made a vague motion toward his face.

"Sick, yeah." He smirked, his half grin laced with scorn. "Guess you could say that."

Her defenses, like hackles, went up, stemming the tears that had threatened to fall. "Grandma's generation sheltered children from the sordid details of life." She snatched her cup to give her hands something to hold on to. Coffee sloshed over and splashed onto the hearth.

"What? No, I ain't fussin' about Granny." He folded the card in half again and slipped it into his back pocket. "I think Granny sat in the hospital with me more than my own mama." He picked up his cup, took a swallow, looking past her shoulder at the wall as he spoke. "My pa'd come 'round, drunk, beat the shit out of me for whatever reason. Mama didn't want to call the sheriff, just stuck me in bed, 'parently waited three days before takin' me to the doctor. Had a high fever. Infection had set in. I came to in the hospital. There was your granny, sittin' by my bed." He paused, smiled. "She'd brought me them root beer barrel candies I liked. And your card."

"I can't believe you kept it all these years."

"Ain't nobody ever made me a card before." He shrugged. "Ain't nobody made me one since."

She swiped at her eyes. "Damn all this dust."

He chugged down the rest of his coffee and then insisted on getting his toolbox and fixing the latch on the back screen door, waving off her objections as she told him not to bother. He went out to his truck; she went back to clearing out the storage space. He came back in, toolbox in one hand, a grocery bag in the other, and headed into the kitchen.

He talked while he worked, mentioned people she didn't know or whose names sounded vaguely familiar. She didn't listen too closely, only gave the occasional generic comment to be polite. He declared the latch fixed, and she thought he'd leave, but he said something about the kitchen clock, followed by the rustle of a plastic bag and a chair being dragged across the linoleum. He asked the time; she consulted her watch and told him.

Surely, he'll go now. But no, he continued to move about the kitchen. A drawer opened, then the rattle of silverware, and something about peanut butter. The earlier emotions which had welled up, the sympathetic feelings which had threatened to overtake her, had long since subsided, were safely sealed away again, and now the presence of another person bothered her, the endless running commentary grated on her nerves and made her skin itch. She just wanted to be alone.

He entered the living room, carrying a chair, and positioned it under the ceiling fan. He switched the fan off and climbed up.

"The best thing to do," he said, "is to take these down. Open up the casing, clean and oil inside. Figure I can do that later. Some WD-

40 oughta be enough for now." He moved on to the parlor, repeated the process. "There," he said as he reentered the room. "I reckon that's better."

While it didn't eliminate the noise, she had to admit the squeaking had reduced considerably. He was extolling the wonders of WD-40 when a sharp *SNAP* came from the kitchen.

"What was that?"

"Mousetrap." He leaned against the doorframe and lit a cigarette. "Pantry done overrun with mice."

Thoughts, like goldfish nibbling at the edges of her mind, began to school together, coalesce. "How'd you know about the mice?"

"Granny's cat run off after she died. He was a good mouser. A big ol' tom. Had a pair like furry ping-pong balls. Figured the mice would've come back." Another trap snapped. "Most folks think mice like cheese, but y'know, they actually prefer peanut—"

"The clock. How'd you know about the clock?" She might've imagined it, but he seemed to pause a bit too long before he answered, fiddling with his cigarette ash.

"Noticed it at the wake," he said. "Battery must've died not too long before, otherwise, your granny would've called me over to change it." He took a long drag, exhaled as he spoke. "Why didn't you come to the wake?"

It was her turn to pause. She went back to shifting through the storage space. "I had to get back to Seattle," she said over her shoulder. "I had appointments the next day."

"Granny'd said you're a doctor, something to do with kids."

"Psychiatrist. I specialize in children, but I see all ages—shit!" A huge spider dashed out in front of her and she jumped, dropping a box marked ORNAMENTS, the contents shattering.

He took a step forward and smashed the spider under his boot. "Damn. That was a big'un. Probably got a nest of them back there." He squatted down to examine it. "Might be a brown recluse. They like dark places. Oughta get you some bug killer, spray along the baseboards." He stood upright, went to the fireplace, and flicked his cigarette ash off. "You want another cup of coffee?"

She didn't and told him so. She opened the box: shards of red, green, silver, and gold glittered inside. *Do they even make glass ornaments anymore?* She folded the flaps and with her foot, slid the box to the wall, the box now destined for the trash.

He came back, sipping a fresh cup of coffee. "I guess you must like kids? Working with kids."

"No, not really. I just try to see that they don't grow up to be sociopaths," she said, speaking without thinking, taken aback by her own honesty. "I mean, I like my job. It's interesting and I think I do some good. I'm just not on a children's crusade." She pulled more stuff out of the space—*Thank God, it's almost empty*—and found a firebox, the key still in the lock. "I appreciate your help, Duncan, really. But I don't want to keep you. I'm sure you have work to do. Elsewhere." Maybe he'd take the hint. She eased herself down to the floor, folding her legs into a half lotus position, her jeans bunching up and pinching behind her knees, and pulled the firebox closer.

"Nah, I took the day off." He wandered around the room, glancing at the piles. "That's a perk of working for yourself. Set your own hours."

She unlocked the box, opened the lid, answered him without looking up. "For some occupations."

"You set your own hours, don't ya?" He poked his toe at one of the open garbage bags next to the recliner. The bag was top heavy and it fell over, spilling some of its contents.

"Not really," she said. The firebox held bundles of papers. *More shit to shift through.*

He set aside his cup and retrieved an old can of shaving cream, its base a ring of rust, that had rolled away. "Me? I work six days a week, mostly. Usually take Sundays off."

The first bundle was her grandfather's life insurance policy. This she set to her left side to be tossed. "What? Did you find Jesus?"

"I dunno. Maybe He found me." He moved around the room, gathering up the scattered items. "Most folks 'round here don't want work done on Sundays anyway. You gotta work Sundays?"

She continued unfolding documents, glancing at them, made quick decisions what to keep or trash. The title to a car that no longer existed—trash. Copies of house papers—keep. Had Duncan said something? She made a non-committal noise. Three birth certificates, her grandfather's, Grandma's, her father's, presented a conundrum. Should she keep them? Her grandparents were dead—why save them? She set them to the right, keeping them just in case.

"You ever watch them crime shows? Those documentaries? They get them doctors, psychiatrists, on there, talking about the killer's mind." He retrieved a half-used tube of hemorrhoid ointment and placed it with the other odds and ends. "Y'know, you should've put the heavier stuff in the bottom. Bag won't fall over that way."

"Tripe," she said. Copies of extended warranties for appliances, long since expired, went on the left.

He picked up and read an almost empty shampoo bottle so old, most of the print had been worn away. He set it aside with the other toiletries. "Yeah, well, hard to understand half of what them doctors say. It's interesting, though, 'specially when they talk about the killer's upbringing. Seems like a crapshoot, having kids. Ain't no tellin' how they'll turn out."

"No, there isn't." She unfolded a half sheet of paper, a Record of Baptism, and a memory grabbed her: she was seven years old, the last

Sunday of the summer before her parents came to take her home, at a congregational picnic on the church grounds, standing in line with the rest of her Sunday school class, waiting her turn, the preacher pinching her nose, his hands stinking of algae, dunking her in the pond behind the church, the preacher's wife giving out small Bibles to the baptized children, powder blue for the boys, pastel pink for the girls, the clamminess of wet clothes clinging to her skin, Grandma wrapping her in an old bedsheet, hugging her close.

She refolded the paper, set it to her left, picked up the next one.

Duncan kept talking. "Lot of them doctors say there were signs. Like when they was little kids, the killers, they'd hurt animals." He paused, eyed Penny sideways. "Or kill them." He shoved his hand into the trash bag, his intention being to take out the lighter items and put the heavy stuff in the bottom for better balance, and his hand brushed against something slick, like a magazine.

The last document in the firebox was her grandparents' marriage certificate. She wavered for a moment: Toss it? Keep it?

He looked inside the garbage bag. Men's clothes, everything balled up and crammed inside, filling the bag, and among the shirts, socks, and trousers, the corner of a magazine peeked through. He pulled it out and then gave a low whistle.

She decided to toss the marriage certificate. She peered down into the bottom of the firebox, her breath caught in her throat.

A sickening mixture of curiosity and repulsion roiled deep and low in his stomach as he stared at the cover: *Barely Legal,* in an outdated, fat-bubbled '60s font, and a close-up of a young woman, her hair up in pigtails and ribbons, eating a Bomb Pop, her lips, wet and glistening, around the cherry-red popsicle tip.

At the bottom of the firebox lay her grandfather's Buck knife. She picked it up. It'd felt so much heavier, had seemed so much bigger, when she was ten. The blade opened easily with a soft *snick*.

He flipped through the pages, his conscience battling with his baser nature. Images flashed of young women dressed up to look like little girls in too short dresses and nightgowns, striking mock innocent poses, revealing shaved pubes. A series of photos featured a petit woman, her hair in braids, her white low-cut blouse barely containing her breasts, a small red-hooded cape around her shoulders, wearing a forest green mini-skirt over a short, frilly petticoat, holding a basket over her arm, seemingly lost in a grove of trees. An old man lurked behind a tree, naked except for a cartoonish wolf mask, his chest and stomach saggy and covered in white hair, a half-assed hard-on hovering over his drooping balls as he leered at the red-caped woman-girl. A few more photographs attempting to convey some type of storyline until the last image: the woman on her hands and knees, head back, eyes closed, her red lips opened in a howl of ecstasy while the old man mounted her from behind like a dog.

Penny turned the knife over in her hand, rubbed her thumb across the wood grain of the handle, tested the tip of the blade with her index finger. Along the flat of the blade, flecks of dried blood dotted the metal surface. Something was caught in the hinge, and she brought the knife closer to look. Three strands of fur, dark at the shaft and tan at the ends.

He'd seen plenty of girlie magazines in his life, but this one soured his stomach, left him wanting a shower, a long, hot shower. Duncan cast a quick, shame-faced glance at Penny's back as he shoved the magazine into the trash bag, pushing it down deep into the tangled bundle of wadded up clothes. Penny sat perfectly still as if she'd been instantly frozen.

He crossed the room, wiping his palms on his jeans, trying to remove a film of filth he felt but couldn't see. "No disrespect, but your pappy was a horn-dog," he said, towering over her. "Whatcha got?"

"His old Buck knife." She looked up at him.

They held each other's gaze, and a memory, unspoken, passed between them.

The silence broke when a brown recluse, huge and heavy with eggs, scurried past Penny, brushed against the skin of her exposed ankle, startling her.

"Damn!" Duncan moved to intercept the spider, stepping into its path. The spider veered to the left, heading toward the fireplace, seeking to escape into the gaps between the bricks. Duncan stepped to the left. The spider dodged. Duncan and the spider danced a spastic waltz among the piles.

"Will you just kill the damn thing already!" she shouted.

The spider swerved but not fast or soon enough. He stomped it, the spider *pop-crunched* under his boot. He lifted his foot. The spider was reduced to a crushed exoskeleton and goo.

"Ha!" His voice held a ring of triumph, and he slid his eyes over to Penny, grinning in his lop-sided way.

She pushed herself up from the floor, folded the knife closed, and slipped it into her back pocket. "You act like you killed a bear."

He shrugged, fished out his cigarettes from his t-shirt pocket. He shook one out and lit it. "You're welcome," he said in an exhale of smoke. When she didn't reply but walked off into the parlor, he called after her. "What?"

She returned with the last remaining liquor box and a pile of newspapers, ignoring him as she went to the fireplace. Knickknacks lined the mantlepiece, and she picked up the nearest one, wrapped it carefully and deliberately in a sheet of newspaper, and placed it in the box. Grandma had loved her knickknacks, and every now and then, a small, unconscious smile would seep across Penny's face when she wrapped ones she'd sent her grandma for birthdays, Christmases, Easters, or just because.

He sauntered over and leaned against the mantle. He picked up a tiny snow globe, shook it, watched the glitter swirl around the miniature city trapped inside. The base of the globe said "Chicago." When the glitter had almost settled, he shook it again. "Granny loved her knickknacks, didn't she?"

Penny's silence was pointed, and a boyish, peevish urge welled up in him to get her attention, the way you want to pet a cat that doesn't want to be touched.

He set the snow globe down. "Hey, you remember Jacko?"

She reached over and snatched up the snow globe. It'd been the last trinket she'd sent to Grandma, bought at a gift shop in O'Hare as she'd waited for her flight back to Seattle after a conference. She wrapped it and placed it in the box.

"Y'know, Jacko? The old preacher's boy? His momma used to let him come over sometimes and play with us?" he said and then went into an agonizingly detailed description of him.

"Yes, okay, damn it! I remember Jacko!" she snapped at him.

"He got bit by a brown recluse. Right on his junk." He gestured at his crotch. "Must've rolled over on one while he was sleepin'."

"That sounds painful," she mumbled.

He chuckled. "'Cept, the idiot didn't go to the doctor. He figured it was a skeeter bite, then when it got all swole up and started turning black, he thought he'd got the clap or somethin'."

Duncan paused, got quiet, waited, blew smoke rings, and watched the rings float up to the ceiling fan where the blades sliced them away.

Finally, in spite of herself, she asked, "Well, what happened? Did he die?"

"Die? Naw. But he waited too long to go to the doctor. They had to cut it off." He made a slicing motion. "Just got a little hole now. Gotta squat like a girl to take a piss." He crushed out his cigarette on the bricks and tossed the butt into the fireplace. "We started calling him 'Jackie.'"

"Why are you here?"

He stepped away, moving to the open trash bag, squatting down to put the spilled items back in the bag, to hell with trying to balance it. "Helping you."

"You're not helping me. You're standing around, jabbering like some damn monkey and chain smoking. That's what you're doing."

He retrieved the last item—a half empty bottle of aftershave—shoved it in the bag and tied off the top as tightly as he could. "Keepin' you company, then."

"I don't want your fucking company!" She snatched up a random knickknack and threw it at him. It missed, smashing against the built-in bookshelves.

He stood, hitching his thumbs in his jeans. "You throw like a girl."

"Go away," she hissed, turning her back on him and grabbing another knickknack. "Or make yourself useful and get some more boxes."

He left without a word.

Once she heard his truck door slam, she went to pick up the broken knickknack. She sat down on the floor and gathered the remnants of what had been a golden-horned unicorn with a heart painted on its chest. An unexpected pang of loss struck her. When she was sixteen, she and her mother had taken a ceramics painting class—a 'mother and daughter bonding' outing prescribed by a family therapist—and she'd picked out the unicorn to paint and send to Grandma for her birthday.

"Maybe I can glue it back together," she murmured, laying the pieces next to each other, like trying to find the corners of a jigsaw puzzle. A piece was missing, leaving a hole in its chest. She scanned the floor but couldn't find it. She pulled her knees up, hugging them close to her chest, and sobbed like a child.

IX

Duncan yanked the truck door open and slam-slid into the driver's seat, cursing under his breath. He pulled the door closed hard enough to rattle the windows and dug out his cigarettes. "Make yourself useful," he muttered as he lit up. He had half a mind to go back in there and tell her off good. Some people were just ungrateful. *She always was spoilt.* Old jealousy welled up in him. As he sat and smoked, swatting at a fly that had buzzed in through the open windows and debating whether or not to go back inside, he heard a cry.

Concern dampened his anger. He eased the door open, slipped out of the cabin, crouch-walked across the gravel driveway and yard until he was under the living room window. He risked a peek. Penny sat on the floor, curled up, hugged her knees to her chest, head bowed and pressed against her thighs, and sobbed, a deep soul cry, like a dam of pain had burst within her.

That's how he had found her that one summer, out in the woods, hugged up and crying, her sundress and hands stained with blood, a dead dog at her feet—one of the stray mongrels that wandered the town—the Buck knife sticking straight up out of its side. He hadn't asked her why she'd done it, had just taken off his shirt and given it to her, told her to wipe off her face and hands while he hid the carcass. *Now you stop cryin',* he'd told her, then took the knife and sliced open his palm, wrapping his bloody shirt around his hand. *There. I'll tell Granny I was messin' around and cut myself.* He'd held her hand, walked her back to the house, and told Granny a lie, taking up the burden of her sin upon himself.

Duncan turned away from the window and walked back to his truck, not bothered if she saw him or not. A heaviness settled on his shoulders. He cranked up the truck and pulled out of the driveway.

X

PENNY PUSHED HERSELF UP FROM THE FLOOR, wiped her eyes with the back of her hands, chiding herself. *Childish.*

She wrapped the broken pieces in a sheet of newspaper, took the bundle into the kitchen and laid it on the counter. A low-grade headache formed behind her eyes. She dug a bottle of aspirin out of her briefcase and washed down two pills with a swig of wine straight from the bottle then poured herself a glass. She ate a slice of cheese. Granny's phone rang. She ignored it. The ringing eventually stopped.

Leaning back against the counter sipping wine, she took stock of what was left to do. A wave of weariness crashed over her, threatening to pull her down, drown her, and she wanted to grab her shit, jump in the car, and leave, fly back to Seattle, pretend Osyka didn't even exist. But there was nothing for it—she had to finish, had to clear out in a few days what Grandma had accumulated over decades. Standing around accomplished nothing. She drained her glass and headed back to the living room.

Two hours had passed when the sound of tires rolling over gravel streamed through the open windows. She stood on one of the kitchen chairs, taking down a pair of ceramic pug-nose dogs from the top bookshelf, wrinkling her nose as her fingers slid over the thick layer of dust that coated the figurines like dirty gray fur. She glanced out the window as the truck came to a stop.

"Son of a bitch." She climbed down from the chair, navigating through the piles of stuff on the living room floor, and crossed into the parlor.

69

She yanked open the front door, stood in the doorway, arms folded tight across her chest, ready to pounce—to tell him to go away, to leave her the hell alone—and waited for him to round the corner. He came into view, but she held her tongue.

"Boxes," he said, taking the porch steps two at a time, and set down four empty liquor boxes. "Wasn't sure how many you wanted. Got more in the truck."

Color rose to her cheeks at the cardboard offerings at her feet. She picked one up. "Thank you."

He grinned and waved it off. "Weren't nothing." He headed back down the stairs.

"Do you need any help?" she called after him.

"Naw," he hollered over his shoulder, "I got it."

She set three of the boxes in the living room entry and started filling the fourth box with newspaper wrapped bundles. He made several trips back and forth, stacking empty boxes against the parlor wall. He'd brought in one last box when she entered the parlor.

"Reckon that'd be enough?" he asked, holding the box out to her.

"More than enough, I'm sure." She leaned forward, peeked into the box he held. "You've got something in there."

He handed off the box to her, reached inside, and pulled out a brown sack. A bottle of Jack Daniel's. "Al, he runs the liquor store, gets pissy if you just get boxes and don't buy nothin'. Thought we'd have a drink later. If you want." He placed the bottle back in the box. "Gotcha some more newspapers in there too. In case you need them."

"Thanks. Where're you going?"

"Got some stuff in the truck."

She placed the whiskey on the kitchen counter—*dear God, I still have to deal with the kitchen*—and took the box with her to the living room. Duncan came through the house, carrying two brown grocery sacks. She raised her eyebrow in a question.

"Ran by the Piggly Wiggly." He passed by her, headed into the kitchen. "Picked up a few things."

"You didn't happen to get trash bags, did you?"

He stuck his head around the corner. "I tried callin', see if you needed anything."

"Sorry," she said. "I thought it might be the preacher again."

He ducked back into the kitchen, laughing. There was the rustle of bags being unloaded and the refrigerator door opening. He asked if she wanted something to drink—a soda or a beer—but she opted for wine, telling him to help himself to wine, if he liked.

Déjà vu came over her when he brought in their drinks, a tumbler of wine for her and a bottle of beer for himself, and they stood in front of the fireplace, leaning against the mantle as they drank.

She pointed at him with her glass. "I thought you'd drink Budweiser."

"I got standards." He took a swing from the bottle, gave the label a passing glance. "Yuengling's pretty good. For a Yankee beer." He set the bottle on the empty mantle to light a cigarette. "I guess you only drink wine?"

To her own surprise, she found herself talking about the various craft beer places in Seattle, the local micro-breweries, and her dislike for IPAs, which he agreed how those tasted like a cross between grass and spoiled grapefruit juice. He told her about a trip he took to the new Lazy Magnolia Brewery, how he'd gone on their brewery and tasting tour, describing the different beers he'd sampled.

The conversation came to a lull, and they stood in a semi-comfortable silence. He finished his beer and looked around the room.

"What'cha gonna do with all this?" he asked.

She followed his gaze, surveying the stacks of papers, piles of trash bags, and the boxes. "What doesn't go to Goodwill, I'll set outside for the garbage pick-up. I only need to keep a few papers."

"Ain't got trash pick-up here," he said. "Gotta take stuff to the dump."

"Shit." She tried to calculate how many trips she'd have to make.

"I can take it for you," he offered. He toed a nearby stack of papers. "Course, a lot of this stuff we could burn."

While he pulled his truck around closer to the front porch and carried out the trash bags, she went back to clearing off the bookshelves, focusing on the assortment of knickknacks and trinkets, then moving on to the variety of board games, their cardboard lids sagging from years of humidity, their corners split from use. There were several framed photos, and some of these she set aside, thinking perhaps her father might like them, even if he couldn't remember who the people were. One photograph she kept for herself, a picture of her and Grandma, standing together on the front porch, arms around each other's waists—she was twelve, nearly as tall as Grandma, and though she hadn't known it at the time, it would be her last summer visit to Mississippi. Pictures of her grandfather she tossed in a pile on the floor.

She had started sorting through the books—mostly religious and inspirational books with some classic works—when Duncan came back inside and poked around in the newly created piles.

"What'cha gonna do with this?" He stood behind the recliner, resting his hand on the back.

She didn't look up from her sorting. "With what?"

"The chair."

"Getting rid of it."

"It's weird," he said. "Granny never let nobody sit in it after your Pappy died."

"Goodwill's supposed to take it. Or, it could go to the dump." The bottom shelf held an encyclopedia set, and she pulled out one of the volumes, opening the cover and consulting the publication date. "You could take this encyclopedia set as well. It's too old to be of any use to anyone."

"Could just burn them."

She shrugged. "Sure. Why not?"

"Chuck 'em in a box. Be easier to carry out." He moved to the side of the recliner, smoothing his hand over the upholstery. An old cigarette burn scratched his palm. "Seems a shame to get rid of this."

She didn't answer him. Encyclopedias filled a box, destined for the fire.

"Y'know what else is kind of weird?" He crouched low, scrutinized the lever mechanism. "Granny never talked much about your Pappy." He straightened up. "But she didn't get rid of none of his stuff."

She needed another box. She stood and headed to the parlor. "Could just take it to the dump. Do you have room in your truck?" she said as she passed by. In the parlor, she grabbed two more boxes from the stack, turned and then stopped, frozen in the doorway.

Duncan sat in the chair. He pulled the lever, and the back of the recliner lowered as the footrest rose. "Still works fine."

The boxes hit the floor with a soft *thud*. "Get out of the chair."

He pushed the lever down, easing the recliner into the upright position. He rubbed his hand against the arm. The upholstery squeaked from the friction. "Fake leather's not a good choice. Get too sweaty in the summer."

She advanced two steps. "Get out of the chair."

"It's tore up some." He picked at a tear. "Could reupholster it. Get a fabric with a cooler nap."

Come sit on Pappy's lap.

"Get out of the fucking chair!"

In the middle of the room she stood, trembling, fists clenched, her fingernails digging into her palms. Hot, painful tears lacerated her eyes. Bile rose up, stuck in her throat, and she covered her mouth, swallowing hard.

"I'm sorry," she said, her voice husky. "I'm so sorry."

He said nothing. He pushed himself out of the recliner and turned away.

"Where are you going?" Her voice was high, scratchy.

He bent over and picked up one of the boxes filled with encyclopedias. "I'm gonna start a fire," he said, and headed into the kitchen, stopping at the fridge to grab a beer. Before heading out the back door, he yelled, "Make a pile of what you want burned." The screen door bounced in the frame, banging shut behind him.

XI

AT THE FARTHEST EDGE OF THE BACKYARD was a fire pit. He dropped the box, the box landed on its side, a couple of encyclopedias slid out onto the ground, and he set down his beer before going off, grabbing a rake and one of the gas cans out of the bed of his truck. He didn't look over at the house at all.

Nothing had been burned in the pit since Granny had died. A few straggly weeds struggled up through the blackened soil and the remnants of the last burn. He took his time raking it out, letting his mind wander between memories and the present. Once the pit was cleared, he dumped the books, poured a bit of gasoline onto the pile, and let it soak in a bit. He tore a flap from the cardboard box, lit it, and touched it to the book pile. The pile ignited with a soft *whoosh*.

He watched the flames, smoked a cigarette, drank his beer, all the while asking himself why he was still there. A glance back at the house gave him the answer. She stood, momentarily, in the doorframe, the outline of her body blurred by the screen. Was she looking at him or simply gazing out? She turned away, her body briefly silhouetted in the kitchen light, and then disappeared.

He poked the fire for something to do. There'd been anger in her voice but something else too, something he tried to put his finger on. It was like that one summer—how old were they? Eight and nine? It'd been a rainy afternoon, and they were running in the house, Granny fussing at them to stop, and Penny'd hit her foot against the coffee table. When he'd asked if she was okay, she screamed at him, saying it was his fault. She'd broken her little toe.

That's how she'd sounded earlier, standing in the middle of the living room, shaking and screaming, anger laced with pain. Like something were broken.

He finished his beer. Near the pit lay a pile of dead wood, and he fed a few sticks and broken branches to the fire, then tossed the empty cardboard box into the flames, and headed back to the house to see what else could be burned.

But when he came through the back porch into the house, she wasn't there. He walked through the living room, the piles of paper and junk unmoved, and he stuck his head into the stairway leading upstairs, calling out her name—no answer except for the sound of running water.

He wandered back into the kitchen and thought about grabbing another beer. A small stack of papers lay on the table, weighted down with a few framed photos. A picture from when Granny was a young woman, some old school photos of Penny's father, another one of Penny as a girl, standing with Granny on the front porch, the two hugging each other's sides—things Penny had set aside earlier. It seemed clear enough what she wanted him to do.

Over the next hour, he hauled stuff out of the living room, taking what could be burned to the fire pit, boxing up the remaining books and items from the bookshelves and stacking these in the parlor with the rest of the things for the thrift store. All that remained in the barren living room was the recliner.

She still hadn't come downstairs; he figured she might be packing up more stuff, though he heard no movement overhead, no creaking floorboards, no footsteps. Maybe she was hiding, like a cat, and if he ignored her, went on about his business, she'd come out in her own time, so he went to tend the fire.

He alternated adding the flammable things from the house with wood from the pile until the fire blazed high, heat radiating, ash and sparks flying upward. The sun had dipped lower in the sky, and the first tree frogs chirped in the trees. He leaned against the rake, listened to the frogs, and watched the flames while memories of past summers rolled through his mind in no particular order. The sun continued its trek toward the horizon, bit by bit, and more frogs joined in the chorus, backed up by cicadas. A lonely firefly sent out a beacon. He flicked his cigarette butt into the fire and then strode across the yard to the house.

He entered the kitchen. Still no sign of her. The grocery sacks he'd brought sat on the counter, and he unloaded them. He moved around the kitchen with a sure familiarity, gathering the can opener, cutting board, a knife, able to lay his hand upon these without having to search. He turned the oven to preheat. From the fridge, he grabbed a beer, a package of thick-cut pork chops, and a slab of fatback. The chops were placed on a plate, seasoned with salt and pepper, and the fatback cut into cubes, half of them into the cast iron skillet to render down. The other half he put in a pot. He fried them for a while, just until the edges started to crisp up, before dumping in a couple cans of green beans.

In between swigs of beer, he cut up potatoes and put them in a ceramic bowl. The fatback in the skillet had rendered down some, and he scooped out a few spoons full of the melted fat over the potatoes, added salt and pepper, and then tossed everything together before spreading the potatoes out, single layer on a baking sheet, which he slid into the oven.

With the green beans simmering on the back burner and the potatoes roasting in the oven, he set about another task, gathering up the broken unicorn, loosely wrapped on the counter, and a tube of super glue he'd bought. He cleared the table, stowing Penny's things on the recliner seat, and spread out several pages of newspaper across the table.

XII

SHE STOOD IN THE MIDDLE OF THE LIVING ROOM, watching Duncan's back as he stomped out of the house, pausing only to grab a beer, a box of encyclopedias tucked under his arm.

"Make a pile of what you want burned!" he yelled, the screen door banging shut behind him.

The piles strewn across the floor mocked her as she tried to sort them, to tame the chaos, until she finally gave up. She grabbed the firebox papers she needed and the pictures she intended to keep and laid these on the kitchen table, weighing down the papers with the framed photos.

When she slipped out into the enclosed porch, she'd meant to go out to Duncan, apologize again, tell him to burn everything left in the living room, but stopped at the outer screen door. He stood, his back toward the house as he watched the flames, occasionally poking at the pit with a rake, the smoke from his cigarette mingling and rising upward with the smoke from the fire.

During her summer visits, when Grandma would burn trash, she'd sometimes let Penny and Duncan tend the fire. The two of them would sit close together, prodding at the fire with sticks, staring at the flames, talking, sharing secrets. But not all secrets.

Shame, like a woolen cloak, weighed down upon her. Her skin itched, felt sticky, grimy, the air close, stifling, hot like a predator's breath, and she wanted—needed—a shower, and she turned away and rushed into the house, not bothering to call out to Duncan.

To hell with it. He'll figure it out.

Upstairs, in the sanctity of the bathroom, she stripped and stepped into the shower, opening the hot water tap on full, the water so hot it took her breath away, and for a time she simply stood under the spray, letting the water sting her face, her body, and then scrubbed herself until her skin glowed an angry pink and the hot water ran out. She shut off the tap. Not bothering to dry off, she headed into the bedroom, leaving a trail of puddled footprints. Drained and light-headed, she dropped, face down, on the bed. She just wanted to rest, to close her eyes for a few minutes.

The sun had lowered when she awoke. Her whole body ached; her muscles, stiff and sore, protested as she sat up. She mentally flogged herself as she dressed—there was too much left to do—and went downstairs.

The state of the living room surprised her. The piles were gone, the built-in bookshelves emptied, the remaining knickknacks nowhere to be seen. She peered into the parlor. Boxes, their flaps folded in on themselves, neatly stacked, lined the parlor wall. Only the recliner remained in the living room. The items she'd had on the kitchen table— her briefcase, photo album, Grandma's big black Bible, the papers, and framed photos—were arranged on the seat.

The aroma of food cooking drew her into the kitchen. The table was set for two. A pot simmered on the back burner, and she lifted the lid for a peek. Green beans with chunks of pork gently bubbled in their own juices, with little pools of fat shimmering on the surface. The glands in the back of her mouth seized up, watered, and she risked burning her fingertips as she plucked a bean out and popped it into her mouth.

The back door opened, footsteps echoed across the porch, and Duncan entered the kitchen, smelling of smoke.

"You're up," he said, moving to the sink to wash his hands. "I was gonna come get you."

She stepped aside, took a tumbler out of the cupboard, and poured herself some wine. Before closing the refrigerator, she grabbed a beer and held it out to him. "You've been busy."

He shrugged and accepted the beer, twisting off the cap and taking a swig, and slid over to the stove. He lit the burner under the cast iron skillet. "You hungry?"

She was. She sat at the table to get out of his way, content to watch him cook. While the fat reheated in the skillet, he checked on the potatoes roasting in the oven, poking them with the tip of a knife, and shut off the oven. When the first wisps of smoke drifted up from the skillet, he laid the pork chops in, the fat sizzling and popping when the meat hit the pan.

She sipped her wine, listened as he made small talk, responding occasionally. He'd been a talker as a boy and, apparently, had never grown out of the habit. *Does he talk to himself when no one's around?*

He tested the pork chops, pressing his fingertip against the meat to determine doneness, then transferred the chops to a clean plate, which he slid into the oven to keep warm while he made gravy. As he spooned flour directly from a bag into the hot rendered lard and stirred it into a bubbling loose paste, he told her how the diner served a halfway decent pork chop and gravy, but, in his opinion, they overcooked the chops and didn't put near enough pepper in the gravy. He poured a steady stream of heavy cream into the roux, whisking until the gravy came together, smooth and thick, added salt, a few dashes of cayenne, and a generous amount of black pepper. He dipped his pinkie into the gravy, tasted it, then shut off the burners and pulled the potatoes and pork chops out of the oven, setting them on the stovetop.

"Here," he said, motioning to her, "hand me your plate."

For a split second, she was going to protest, insist she could fix her own damn plate, but she didn't and handed over her plate as asked. If only to herself, she had to admit there was something homey, comforting, sitting in the kitchen, watching him cook, being tended to, served—the feeling of being safe and warm, like a child with no knowledge of good and evil.

After filling her plate and his own, he sat down across from her. She waited while he bowed his head, assuming he offered a quick, silent prayer of grace, and then they both dug in. For several minutes, they were quiet, focused on their food, the only sounds were of silverware clinking against the plates. She couldn't remember the last time she'd eaten something so filling.

"The chops are good." She paused for a sip of wine. "Almost as good as Grandma's."

He chuckled. "Guess I didn't use enough of her 'secret ingredient,'" he said, pointing toward the stove with a quick tip of his head.

She turned, scanning where he'd indicated. On the back of the stove sat the ceramic shaker with "Love" written on it. How many times, as a child, had she sat at the table on a summer night, watching Grandma cook, and before anything was set on the table, Grandma would shake "Love" over everything?

Penny looked away, focused on her plate. "You mustn't have." She wiped her nose with a paper towel. "You definitely used plenty of pepper, though."

If he noticed the color rising on her throat and cheeks or the glimmer of tears in the corner of her eyes, he chose to say nothing. Instead, he grinned and stabbed a forkful of green beans. "Lord, do you remember her fried chicken?"

A memory-fueled conversation about Grandma's cooking flowed easily between them, one remembered dish prompting the memory of another, reminiscences of congregational summer picnics on the church grounds where each lady secretly hoped to "win" by having the most praised food offering, how Grandma often "won" the coveted prize of praise in these covert contests. The conversation moved naturally to food and cooking in general; Duncan humble-bragged about his cooking abilities; Penny laughed through the retelling of the first and only dinner party she'd hosted, which had failed miserably in the food department, but she'd made sure everyone had plenty of wine.

The conversation lulled, their plates empty.

He pushed a stray chunk of fatback around the plate with his fork. "Why'd you stop comin' down?"

She scooted her chair back, crossed her legs. "My parents divorced."

"Yeah, I knew that. Granny told me." He eased his chair back and lit a cigarette. "Still don't explain why you stopped visitin.'" He blew a stream of smoke toward the ceiling. "I used to look forward to you comin.' Like Christmas."

"It was decided that I'd live with my mom. My mom thought my summers would be better spent at expensive, fancy-ass, all-girl camps. Structured recreation and all that." While she spoke, she folded her paper towel over and over on her thigh.

"I thought, maybe, they'd found out...y'know...down by the pond."

Her last summer, a hot, lazy day, the high noon heat oppressive, the humidity suffocating, and they'd ran to the pond to sit on the edge of the short pier, to dip their feet into the tepid green water, seeking some relief—which one of them had suggested skinny-dipping? Whoever had suggested it, the other had agreed. They'd slipped out of their clothes, sneaking glances at each other, curious of and embarrassed by their adolescent bodies, and jumped into the obscurity of the pond, the algae-tinted water covering their nakedness. A clumsy, fumbling first kiss, hands moving, exploring, hidden by the murky water. Along the rural road, high on the embankment, someone walked with their dog, the dog running and rushing ahead, barking and yapping in excitement, and their hearts had stopped as they scrambled out of the pond and into their clothes and dashed away, hand in hand, praying they hadn't been seen.

Penny couldn't remember how, or even if, she had explained her wet hair to Grandma. "I don't know." She picked up her tumbler and swirled the last swallow around. "Grandma never said anything."

He traced a ring of condensation with his fingertip. "We had somethin', didn't we?"

"Duncan, we were children. We didn't 'have' anything," she said, not unkindly. She drained her glass and stood. "Let's get the dishes done, so I can pack up the kitchen."

While he cleared the plates, she retrieved empty boxes from the parlor and set them on the table. He washed. She dried and packed. She told him to keep the cast iron skillet, if he wanted it. He did.

After the dishes were cleaned and packed away, they emptied the cupboards and drawers, keeping out a few items she'd need the next day. They carried the boxes away and stacked them with the others. He asked if she wanted a drink. She did. Once again they stood by the fireplace, leaning against the mantle, sipping Jack and Coke.

"I guess Pastor Jones invited you to church tomorrow," he said.

"He did." She took a sip of her drink—heavy on the Jack, light on the Coke.

"You goin'?"

She snorted. "Hell no."

He laughed, fished out his cigarettes, and lit one.

They drank, at first exchanging small talk, but then slipping into an easy silence. Through the open windows, night sounds filtered in, frogs croaking and crickets chirping, the distant hooting of an owl, the occasional car driving by. Moths battered against the screens, seeking ingress, drawn to the wan indoor light. He concentrated on blowing smoke rings toward the ceiling; she watched the fan blades slice through them. She went to take a sip of her drink but found the glass empty.

"I hate to ask you this," she said, clinking the ice around in her glass, "but somebody needs to be here Monday. Goodwill's supposed to collect the rest of the furniture. Could you—"

"Sure, no problem. What time?"

"'Before noon.' Whatever that means. But I've got an early flight."

"Yeah, I can be here."

"They *should* take everything."

"I'll drop off whatever they don't take."

A smile, genuine and rare, bloomed across her face. "Thanks." She paused, glancing around the empty space. "And...I appreciate you coming over and helping. Making dinner..."

"T'weren't nothin'," he said, grinning and shrugging. "Happy to help."

She traced the rim of her glass, staring at the melting ice. "Sorry I was so...rude, ugly, earlier."

"Don't worry about it." He risked reaching out and stroked her arm. "I imagine it was hard goin' through all this stuff. Memories and all that."

"Yeah." Her eyes fell upon the recliner. "Memories."

He finished his drink and placed his glass on the mantle. "I suppose I oughta get goin'."

"Sure." She gave herself a little shake, as if a chill rippled through her. "I got to get an early start tomorrow. Still have things to sort through."

He nodded toward the recliner. "Reckon you can help get that in the truck?"

She gathered her things from the recliner seat—briefcase, photo album, the framed pictures and papers, Grandma's Bible. Without thinking, she picked up the Bible by its spine; a mass of papers, pamphlets, and clippings slipped out and fell to the floor, leaving a trail as she carried everything into the kitchen.

He pushed the recliner then paused. Among the grime and dust bunnies lay something small and white and he bent over to pick it up—a fragment from the broken ceramic unicorn, a tiny red heart painted on the white surface. He slipped it into his pocket and moved to help her collect the papers.

"D'you see this?" He held out an envelope with Penny's name written across the front in Granny's fine, spidery scrawl.

She took it. "I'd forgotten about this." She tore off the end and pulled out the contents. One sheet of paper folded into thirds—a letter from Grandma, dated the day before she died. The sheet shook in her hands.

He moved behind her, so close she sensed the air compress between their bodies, felt his breath, warm and moist, on her neck as he read over her shoulder.

"Damn," he whispered.

As still and unmoving as Lot's wife, Penny stood, transported beyond time and space, no longer seeing the paper in her hand or the room. Emotions roiled and clashed—guilt and peace, shame and relief, sadness and joy—and a memory, long-buried and ignored to the point of forgetting, resurfaced and played in a Technicolored clip on the screen of her mind until the screen went blank and one sentence, bright against the black void, burned hot and white:

I killed your Pappy.

She opened her eyes, back in the present, in the room, in herself, her hands steady, the paper still, Duncan's whispered "damn" brushing against her neck, his breath laced with a lingering hint of whiskey.

"Duncan?" she said, turning her face toward the recliner. "Will that burn?"

XIII

SHE SAT ON THE BACK PORCH STEPS, watching the fire, the wind picking up and blowing the chemical stench away from the house, and waited for Duncan to bring her a drink. They had hauled the recliner to the fire pit. The earlier fire had died down, and he'd raked the coals smooth and centered the recliner in the pit. When he'd stepped aside, she'd taken the Buck knife and slashed the upholstery with an unsettling ferociousness, shredding the faux leather to ribbons. Bits of foam and stuffing whirled around like snow flurries, and she'd spewed profanities as if possessed—cursing, railing, and wailing until her voice had given out. She flung the knife onto the seat, and he dosed the ruined chair with gasoline. She'd twisted Grandma's letter into a tight roll, and he lit the end with his lighter. She dropped it on the seat. At first, it'd appeared as if nothing would happen, the small flames flickering, hesitant, but then fire sparked, spread, the ribbons of upholstery catching and curling; thick acrid smoke gathered and billowed upward. He'd taken a step back, coughing, but she had stood, staring down the blaze, the heat pushing against her, flames swiping at her, threatening to scorch her, consume her, until he'd reached out, grabbed her arm, pulled her back. He'd led her back to the porch by the hand. She hadn't resisted, allowed herself to be guided to the steps, nodded her head when he'd asked if she wanted a drink.

"If there is a hell," she whispered to the darkness, "I hope you're there."

The screen door opened. Duncan came out, two glasses in one hand, the bottle of whiskey in the other. He eased himself down close beside her.

"Here." He handed her the glasses and poured a generous two-fingers into each, placing the bottle nearby.

She mumbled 'thanks.' For a time they drank in silence, staring at the flames, their thighs touching.

He cleared his throat. "You wanna talk about it?"

"What?"

"Ain't that what you people do? Talk about shit?" He shook out a cigarette and offered it to her.

She accepted it, leaned in closer so he could light it, and took a long drag, exhaled, watched the smoke as it plumed and dissipated into the heavy humid night air.

"No," she said, taking another drag. "I'll see my therapist next week. That's what I pay her for."

He chuckled. "A shrink seeing a shrink." Puffs of smoke punctuated his words. "That's rich."

They drank more whiskey, smoked more cigarettes, and said very little as they sat late into the night, keeping a vigil on the fire. A summer storm front moved in. Thick clouds rolled across the sky, blocking out the moon. Fat raindrops, like warning shots, spattered, pinging off the tin roof, then it came down, fast and steady like a shower opened on full. The rain struck the ground, bounced and ricocheted, dampening their legs. Static built up, charged the air, raised the fine hairs on their arms. A bolt of lightning crackled across the sky; a clap of thunder boomed close behind, rattling the roof. He suggested going inside. She shifted, faced him head on. When she leaned in and kissed him, full on the mouth, neither one of them could've said who was more surprised.

They ended up in her grandma's bed, the bedframe creaking, the headboard knocking rhythmically against the wall, their bodies entwined upon the stripped down mattress, fucking over and over until they were empty and spent.

Afterward, they sat up in bed, Duncan propped up on pillows against the headboard, Penny leaning back against his chest, and shared a cigarette, using a glass as a makeshift ashtray, talked about nothing in particular, the conversation meandering, pausing and picking up again, as if they'd always spent Saturday evenings in bed together. They had each other once more before sleep could no longer be avoided. They stretched out, side by side, Duncan smoothing his palm over her thigh, Penny stroking the hair on his chest and stomach.

"Y'know what we could do?" His voice was heavy and languid, on the verge of sleep. "Turn this place into a bed 'n breakfast."

She didn't answer; he had drifted off.

XIV

BEFORE DAWN, she slipped out of bed and picked her clothes off the floor. Duncan slept on his back, one arm over his head, the other across his stomach. He didn't stir.

She tiptoed across the hall into the bathroom, brushed her teeth, and ran a brush through her hair before collecting her toiletries and padding down the hallway to her father's old bedroom. She put on clean clothes, gathered and shoved the rest of her things into her carry-on, slung her purse over her shoulder, left the room, and snuck downstairs.

The sun had not yet risen, the sky cloaked in gray, the night's rain temporarily taming the humidity. Ozone lingered in the air. She placed her carry-on and purse by the front door.

In the kitchen, she retrieved a few items from the table and slipped them into her briefcase. She tore a sheet of paper from a legal pad, scribbled a brief note, then folded the page in half. On the front, she printed his name and weighted it down on the table with the salt shaker. She left the kitchen, walked through the house, and out the front door.

In the rental car, she dug the GPS out of the glove box, plugged it in, and punched in the address for the Louis Armstrong New Orleans International Airport. She glanced at her watch—the ticket counter should be open by the time she'd arrived—and pulled out of the driveway. She didn't look back.

XV

HE WOKE UP AND KNEW SHE WAS GONE. Not just up and out of bed, but gone as in left. The house felt empty. He sat on the edge of the bed, stretched, then got up and pulled on his jeans. He grabbed his cigarettes and lighter off the nightstand and bent to scoop up his shirt and boots as he left the bedroom and headed downstairs. At the bottom of the stairs, he dropped his boots and shirt to the floor, strode through the living room and into the kitchen, flipping on the light.

"Could've at least made a pot of coffee 'fore you headed out." He lit a cigarette, grinning to himself as he measured out coffee grounds, filled the carafe, poured the water into the machine, and switched it on. While he waited for the coffee to brew, he leaned back against the counter, sipped a glass of water, and glanced around the kitchen. His gaze stopped at the table. She'd left some things—the photo album and some papers. He set the glass down and moved to the table for a closer look.

There was a folded sheet of paper with his name printed on it, held down with the salt shaker. He removed the shaker and picked up the note, letting his cigarette dangle from the good corner of his mouth, squinting against the smoke as he held the note in both hands and read it. Twice.

"Damn," he said. He placed the note on the table, took a long drag off his cigarette, slipping his hand into his pocket. Something hard, like a pebble, brushed against his fingertips. "What the hell?" He pulled the object out.

Behind him, the coffee pot gurgled and spat out the last drops of coffee. He turned the small, red and white object over in his palm, then smiled in recognition—the shard from the broken unicorn. The last piece needed to make it whole again.

Acknowledgments

Thank You, Abba, for this wonderful and terrifying gift.

About the Author

M.S. Gardner moves between the worlds of fabulism and realism and draws inspiration from the curious, bizarre, and absurd nature of life. She's perfected her impersonation of a normal human being well enough to hold a job at a local library. While her physical body resides on the Alabama Gulf Coast, she mostly lives in her head.

Her work has also appeared in *That Is TOO Wrong! An Anthology of Offbeat Horror Vol. 2*, *The Dead Mule School for Southern Literature*, *Psychopomp*, *Terror House Magazine*, *Coastal Shelf*, *Running Wild Story Anthology Vol. 5*, *Page & Spine*, *Hypnopomp*, *Altarworks*, and *Strangelet Journal*.

Comparable April Gloaming Titles

The Four Deaths of Clayton Standard by Josh Patrick Sheridan

The Author Project by Malaika Favorite

The House That Wasn't There by Andrew Forrest Baker

Ash Tuesday by Ariadne Blayde

We Never Took a Bad Picture by Ashley N. Roth